THE UNTANGLING OF TWO HEARTS

BEAR CREEK BRIDES BOOK THREE

AMELIA ROSE

CONTENTS

This book is dedicated to all of my faithful readers, without whom I would be nothing. I thank you for the support, reviews, love, and friendship you have shown me as we have gone through this journey together. I am truly blessed to have such a wonderful readership.

CHAPTER 1

*I*t was happening again. His rage and anger washed over her before he eventually slapped her across the face with the back of his hand. She'd felt this anger before, had been confused by it, afraid of it, and now tired of it. As she hit the ground, the smell of whiskey thick in the air, she quickly pushed herself back onto her feet and made a dash for the kitchen door.

His slurred words followed her as she disappeared into the shadows of the alleyway. The neighbor's house was only ten feet away from their shack of a home, but she'd learned from past experiences that if she fled to their house, they'd only send her home. These faithful Christian believers had told her that all children had to obey their parents, no matter what. Therefore, Nancy ran for the shadows where her father wouldn't be able to find her in his drunken stupor. No one would be able to find her as she hid amongst the young oak trees.

Nancy pressed her body low to the ground, her head reeling from the pain of the slap as her father stumbled out of the kitchen door of what she used to consider their home. He held a lantern out before him, trying to spot any signs of his daughter. Squinting his eyes didn't help as he moved the lantern from side to side, hoping to push back the shadows and catch any sign of her. She couldn't have gotten far and would have to come home eventually.

"I know yer out there!" he cried into the night, not caring who else heard him. Their home was positioned at the end of a side street that paired off from the main road into town. When he'd first purchased the house, he thought himself lucky to be living so close to town. But as their lives progressed, and things continued to only get worse, he realized that this part of town was considered where all the poor, no good families lived. It was just one more prejudice the town's people had placed on him, and he was growing very tired of them, and everyone else.

"You get back here and finish cooking me dinner the way I like it!" he shouted again.

With every shouted word that swept through the small alley-way, Nancy cringed. There was no way she was going to go back into that kitchen and try to appease her father. It's not like he ate that much anymore; he preferred to drink the night away. She wasn't sure what bug had bit him today, but she could tell the moment she got home from her shift at the general goods store that her father was in a particularly bad mood. And the instant he got a chance, he began to take his frustrations out on her. Normally he just yelled, making Nancy feel small and very much unloved and unwanted. But tonight he'd resorted to what Nancy feared the most, and that was being on the receiving end of many of his punches.

As she lay on the ground, praying the young oak tree would protect her from her father's lantern, she could already feel her face swelling from the impact of the backhanded blow to her face. She prayed that her right eye wouldn't swell shut so she could get to work tomorrow morning. Nancy needed every penny she could collect in order to escape Indiana and any influence her father had over her. She'd learned that no one was willing to come to her rescue, no matter how many times she showed up at work with a black eye or a bloody nose. It was clear to see that she was being abused at home, but it seemed like nobody cared.

This whole experience had taught Nancy that the only person she had in the world was herself. She'd been working hard for years to save up enough money to leave her hometown. Once, her father found her stash of money underneath her mattress in her bedroom when he was in an angry fit and had turned it over instead of hitting her. Ever since then, Nancy had to work even harder to keep her money hidden and safe from her father. He'd grown even more suspicious of her and had accused her of lying to him from that day forth.

After a while, her father gave up shouting for her and trying to spot her in the darkness. He went back inside, the lantern light disappearing behind the kitchen door he slammed shut. Nancy was thankful that at least it was a warm night on the backend of summer. The warm months were swiftly falling away to fall, and Nancy didn't want to be around for another cold winter, trapped inside her house.

When she felt like it was finally safe, she eased her way out from underneath the tree and righted herself. She brushed any dirt or dust off her day gown, hoping it would be presentable enough for tomorrow since she didn't have many gowns and hardly had time to do her own laundry. Slowly, she made her way behind all the houses on the street towards the communal well. There, she quietly pulled up a bucket of water and used her handkerchief to wash her face and hands before trying to clean up her gown. She cupped her clean hands and drank as much water as her belly would handle before lowering it back down into the well.

Having nowhere else to go, and not wanting to chance her father was still awake and not yet passed out from all his drinking, Nancy wandered through the back yards of the houses till she came upon the main street of the town. Here, most businesses and houses had lanterns resting on the front doorways and porches to show newcomers what was available. Nancy slowly walked along the boardwalk in front of all the businesses, peering into windows and trying to unstiffen her body with a bit of exercise.

As she neared the local saloon, Nancy could hear music being played from an upright piano. She'd only ever been in the saloon once, having convinced herself that she could make more money as a dancing girl. Her fire-red hair and bright green eyes often got her plenty of attention from unwanted men. She figured she'd be good at it and could earn a lot more than what she was being paid to dust shelves at the general store. But the moment she'd stepped into that place and took a good look around, she knew that she could never get on a stage dressed in a revealing way in front of all those lusty men. She might be desperate, but she wasn't that desperate.

A warm breeze blew through town and Nancy closed her eyes, imagining it was a comforting sign that everything would be alright. She was startled when a sheet of newspaper came colliding with her, the sound of it hitting her gown causing her eyes to pop open to see what had happened. She quickly grabbed the newspaper before it could blow away and figured that she'd try her hand at reading. Nancy didn't have much education, but enough to read and write simple things and do a bit of mathematics.

As Nancy continued walking at a leisurely pace, she read

through the newspaper, glad that her eye had only swollen a little. She could see clearly as she walked and read over different news articles and advertisements. She even caught sight of a few mail-order-bride ads and wondered why she'd never considered replying to any of them before.

Nancy's heart started to pound in her chest as she thought of a most thrilling idea. What if she went to meet one of these men? She could have a way to start over and live a happier life. She could get as far away from Indiana as she wanted to and never have to worry about returning because she'd be properly married and could have a home of her own. Nancy knew that she had many housekeeping skills and could make any man happy. *Then why not*, she wondered as she read through all the advertisements.

She didn't have high standards when it came to reviewing the mail-order-bride ads. She simply wanted to get as far away from Indiana as she could and marry a man who was kind and caring. More than anything, Nancy wanted someone she could fall in love with who would equally love her that much in return. She knew that she was pretty and charming, she simply needed to feel the love she was never given in her life.

There was one particular ad that caught her attention. Nancy stopped in front of a shop and held the newspaper up to the lantern light to get a closer look at the words. She read them and saw the town and territory from which the ad had been placed. She'd never heard of the town before and figured it would be the perfect place to disappear to. Plus, the author of the ad sounded quite caring and interested in marrying as soon as possible. Nancy liked the sound of that as she carefully tore the ad from the paper before folding it up and putting it into her underskirt pocket.

With a plan in mind, Nancy made her way back to her home.

She pressed her ear up against the kitchen door, listening for any sounds that her father was still awake. Taking a deep breath, Nancy carefully pushed open the door and took a quick peek around the door. The lantern was still on, filling the space with plenty of light. Nancy took a few steps into the house, listening for any sign of her father. She picked up the lantern off the kitchen counter and started to walk carefully into the house.

As she rounded the kitchen corner and stepped into the main room of the house, she spotted her father's slumped form on the cushioned chair he often took to after drinking too much to make it to his bed. He sat there with his head slung over the back of the chair as he snored softly. Nancy stood still for several moments, waiting to see if he would wake back up. She'd left the back door open and could flee if he suddenly awoke and tried to come after her again. But when she was certain he wasn't waking up any time soon, she carefully continued on to her bedroom down the hallway.

With the bedroom door closed and locked, Nancy was quick to set down the lantern on her dresser and pull out her only trunk. She didn't have many things, therefore it didn't take her long to pack. And inside the lining of the trunk was all the money she'd been squirreling away for months. Everything was set to go, she'd only ever needed a destination. And since she knew of a man in need of a wife in a town very far, far away, she was eager to go out and meet him right away before any other woman decided to write him.

Once Nancy was packed and ready for her great escape, she blew out the lantern and waited for her eyes to adjust to the darkness. She wouldn't be able to carry her trunk and the lantern and knew that she'd need to navigate the house with her arms full and her eyes practically blind. But she'd snuck around the house in the dark plenty of times to either sneak some food at night to fill her belly or get the mending supplies to fix her gowns. Her father was a very cheap man and barely let her eat more than he deemed proper for a young lady or use materials that he thought were unnecessary.

As carefully as Nancy could with her arms full, she made her way out of her room and tiptoed down the hallway. She thought she was breathing too loudly as her heart beat frantically in her chest. This was the moment she'd been preparing for all her life and now that the moment had come, she was terrified. She was pleading with the Good Lord silently in her mind as she made her way through the house. Before she'd been so confident sneaking past her father while he lay unconscious from drinking so much. But with so much riding on her getting out of the house before he woke up, she was sweating hard as she made her way through the main room.

Nancy was grateful that at least she'd left the kitchen door open for when she approached it, all she had to do was step right out without having to do a thing. As the night greeted her once more, Nancy could hardly believe that she'd done it. Her father hadn't woken up and caught her leaving, nor had she made any mistakes thus far. Now all she had to do was get her horse and make it to the closest train station.

Nancy walked all the way through town to the other side where the livery stables were. Though it was technically her father's horse, she had been the one to pay for the mare and keeping the horse well-fed and exercised by the stable hands. Walking into the large barn was a thrilling feeling for Nancy because she knew at this point, she was practically free.

She didn't bother waking up any of the stable hands as she walked down the row of horse stalls till she found Blondie. Nancy set down her trunk, the strain of the weight of the trunk leaving her arms quickly as she then found a lantern and lit it.

She then got to work getting her mare saddled so she could start her grand adventure.

"What'cha doing, Miss Nancy?" came a low, male voice from behind her. Nancy swirled on her feet as she gasped, her fears rising quickly.

"What'cha think I'm doing, Billy?" Nancy asked when she noticed Billy Turner, the son of the man that owned the livery stables. His face looked sleepy and she knew she'd woken him.

"Looks like you're taking Blondie here for an evening ride," Billy said as he looked at her and then looked at the trunk on the ground. "You going to need help securing that trunk?"

"I'd be mighty obliged," Nancy said as she led Blondie from the stall and into the light of the lantern to finish getting her ready. Billy sighed and helped Nancy finish the work, and together they got the trunk on the back of Blondie and fastened it down with plenty of rope. As Nancy then went to pull herself up into the saddle, Billy placed his hand on her forearm, stopping her. Nancy looked at Billy, worried if he was going to try and stop her.

"I really hope I never see you again," Billy said with a smile. He lifted his hand and lightly touched the spot on her face that was still tender from being struck. Nancy flinched away from his touch.

"I assure you that the feeling is mutual, Billy. You take care of yourself now. And for the love of God, don't tell anyone you saw me tonight," Nancy said as she pulled herself up into the saddle.

"Couldn't see nothing if I was asleep in my bed all night," Billy replied as he took several steps back so Nancy could clear the barn. Once up in the saddle, her legs positioned side-saddle, Nancy nodded once to Billy as he went down to the end of the stable and opened up the gate for her. She then steered Blondie in that direction and put her into a trot as they made their way out.

Once Nancy left the stables and headed out of town, she didn't look back. She didn't look over her shoulder to see if Billy was standing there, watching her ride out of town. She didn't look around to see if her father had surprisingly awoken and was now looking for her frantically. All she did was keep an eye on the road leading out of town, using the moonlight to guide her, and all her hopes and dreams to motivate her to ride through the night. She was finally free to chase down her own destiny and secure a better future for herself.

CHAPTER 2

*D*an sat at his desk in the town hall. Before him were the many sets of pews for when his students would come in and complete their daily lessons. The building was, of course, used for town meetings, and at least one Sunday out of the month Pastor Munster came through and delivered a sermon in the same space. Bear Creek, Montana wasn't a big town by any stretch of the imagination. It had everything a person would need and not too much more. As the town's schoolteacher, Dan was in charge of instructing the children and teaching them the basics of reading, writing, and mathematics. But with the harvest season soon approaching, he knew that the majority of his students wouldn't be making an appearance till after the harvest was completed.

It was currently late afternoon, his students having just left for the day in a rambunctious group, all ready to return home. Dan loved working with the children and was glad to see that most of them were progressing nicely in their lessons. A few he had to work extra hard with to teach them their letters and how to pronounce words. Most of them would grow up to be farmers just like their fathers, or cattle ranchers, or some other family position. But Dan was hopeful that a few might pursue a higher level of education to either become a doctor or a lawyer. With Dr. Harvey being a much older man now, the town could use another doctor and some sort of legal representation.

At this moment, Dan wasn't worried about his students or the current happenings of the town. He tutored a few adults in improving their reading and writing skills, but that wasn't scheduled till tomorrow. And the reading group he'd started up wasn't meeting again until later in the week. What Dan was focused solely on were the few letters that lay on his desk presently. Dan ran a few fingers through his short brown hair. Then, he rubbed his jaw and realized that he'd gone a few days without shaving once more. Sometimes Dan would get in too much of a rush to make sure he was at the town hall before his students arrived that he forgot to shave or have a good meal in the morning.

Dan picked up the first letter and pulled at the seal till it gave way. Then, he unfolded the sheet of writing paper and read the short, few sentences from whichever woman had decided to write him. Dan was always optimistic each time he received a letter from someone who had written in reply to his mail-order-bride ad. He was very much in want of a wife and couldn't exactly find anyone local. The town had been developed when the mines opened up in the mountains. It was a town ran by men for men. Not too many women were present unless they were already married. And since more men had started to marry mail-order-brides in Bear Creek, to include the town's sheriff, Dan thought he'd give a good shot at it.

But Dan sighed heavily as he folded up the letter and set it aside. It was another, "I cook, I clean, I'm fertile," letter that didn't appeal to him at all. Dan was certain that any woman could be taught to keep house or cook, much like Jenny Jenkins had learned with her mother, Margret, when they'd come to town. Jenny had replied to Mathew Jenkins' mail-order-bride ad, but being city dwellers, they had a lot to learn about living in the country. Therefore, Dan was positive that women could be taught these things and therefore hadn't made it a requirement in his ad. Yet, women still continued to write to him in this manner, making him think that all women cared about was a roof over their heads and a husband to please.

Dan opened the next letter, always trying to remain hopeful and positive. He read the short letter, sighing heavily when it followed a similar format to the rest. He folded it up as well and moved on to the next one. Though Dan had received plenty of responses, often receiving a dozen letters each week, he had yet to read a letter that piqued his interest. He wanted a wife whom he could not only love, but respect and adore. He knew that it would be hard to find a woman who matched his intelligence, but if he could at least meet someone who was at least interested in the same things that interested him, he could overlook any lack in education or comprehension.

The more he thought about what type of woman he would like to marry one day, the image of someone he'd started to become familiar with rose in his mind. There was one particular woman that attended his reading group that had certainly piqued his interest. She not only could comprehend the themes and tropes of the books they'd been studying, but also had her own, unique perspective of why the author decided to construct the book in that particular way. While most of the reading group members would comment on the pleasantness of the books he chose for the group to read, Phoebe James on the other hand always had more to say and comment on. It was her intelligence that really drew Dan to her, even though Phoebe was a beauty as well.

Dan didn't know too much about Phoebe outside her interest in books. He knew that her older brother, Edward James, had purchased the mines almost three years ago. Ever since then, the mines had been successful, making Dan curious to why Edward had succeeded while previous mine owners had not. Dan liked mysteries and often thought of this one in his spare time.

Dan also knew that Phoebe and Edward James came from a respectable family in Boston. At least, that's what Mathew and Jenny Jenkins had told him over dinner one evening. They first met the siblings the day of their marriage. The wedding reception had been at the inn where the siblings had been staying upon arriving to Bear Creek. There, Mathew and Jenny learned about the two. Dan was curious about Phoebe and her past, wanting any excuse to talk to her personally.

But that is where Dan's problems started. He was often nervous around Phoebe because he knew that he liked her but didn't know how to go about sharing his feelings. He was afraid she'd reject him because he was a simple schoolteacher and not a gentleman like what she was probably used to in Boston. And furthermore, Phoebe had made it quite clear that she wasn't interested in marriage. Dan wasn't the only single man in Bear Creek that was interested in courting Phoebe. She was really the only available option when it came to choosing someone to marry in their area. But with every offer Phoebe received, Dan only heard of her rejections time after time.

After giving up on any hope that he could be the one to win over Phoebe's heart, he'd decided to place a mail-order-bride ad. He was hoping to meet someone from the East who perhaps had the same higher education as he had and could keep up a good conversation with him. Realistically, he wanted to meet someone like Phoebe who was intelligent and witty, who could read a book and see the overall themes and messages the author wanted the reader to understand instead of just seeing it as a good book to read. He wasn't sure if this was even possible anymore because the majority of women who had written him didn't seem to hold any of these characteristics. Not even one.

Dan was throwing the stack of opened letters into the waste bin as footfalls sounded in the town hall. He looked up from his desk expecting to see the town's mayor, Mr. Demetri Franklin, on his way out for the day. The man always greeted Dan in the morning and afternoons. But he was pleasantly surprised to instead see two-year-old Mikey Jenkins toddling up the aisle with his parents close behind him.

"The Jenkins family," Dan said happily as he stood from his desk. "I believe it's a bit early for Mikey to be attending school." Mathew and Jenny chuckled as they came near. Dan bent down and collected Mikey in his arms, tickling him to hear the small child laugh.

"You've always been so good with children," Jenny said as she collected her son and held him on her hip. He could clearly see that Jenny was expecting again as her middle continued to grow. He was happy for the family and hoped they would have continued prosperity.

"It is partially why I became a schoolteacher," Dan replied. "I do love being around the children and teaching them all sorts of fun things besides the basics."

"And what is the other part of why you wanted to be a schoolteacher?" Mathew asked with a smile. His hair was growing longer again and Dan wondered if he was going to have Mitchel Franks, the local barber, cut it for him.

"I didn't want to be a farmer like my father. I enjoyed books too much to spend my days and nights out in the fields. Though I do appreciate everything a farmer, and cattle rancher, does for this community," Dan said, knowing that Mathew had become a successful cattle rancher over the last few years. Mathew had continued on his father's ranch, much like his father had done before him. And Dan knew that Mathew took great pride in his work. He'd even doubled the size of his herd and had several cattle hands to help him. If Dan was correct, Mathew had the largest herd in the area.

"Speaking of books, I wanted to say that my mother dearly loves the selections you pick for the book club. She enjoys attending the meetings every week, and I always think it's good for her to get out of the house and socialize more," Jenny spoke up. "She's a wonderful grandmother, but I want her to have a life, too."

Dan smiled with the memory of Margret Phillips, Jenny's mother. The woman laughed easily and was always a joy to be around. She was also a hard worker, cleaning for several of the businesses in town. Though Dan was certain that Margret didn't need to work for financial stability, it seemed the older woman simply liked the task and the ability to socialize as she worked.

"I'm glad to hear your mother is enjoying the books. We should be finished with the current novel in a few weeks and I've started to think of what the group might be interested in reading next."

"Well, I'd like to say this is a personal visit. Though we've come to town to make some purchases for the ranch, we've also come on behalf of Brown Bear," Mathew explained. Dan's eyebrows furrowed together, having not expected that an Indian chief would ever want to send him a message.

"Alright. What does the Sioux leader want?" Dan asked tentatively. He was curious, but also a little worried. It wasn't that he didn't like Indians. He just wasn't sure of them, nor had he spent a lot of time around the local Indian tribe. He knew that Mathew was very close with Brown Bear, and that the Indian leader had done the town a great service when his people came down from the mountains to provide medical aid when a terrible cough broke out in town a few years ago and took the lives of a few men. Therefore, Dan knew that the Indians were no trouble. He simply wasn't used to them personally.

"Brown Bear understands that this country is progressing towards a different future. His people and other Indian tribes are being forced to abandon their traditional way of life. And in order for his people to continue surviving, he knows that change needs to happen. Therefore, he has requested to meet with you and discuss the possibility of you teaching the Indian children English, to read and write it."

Dan stared at Mathew for a moment, letting his words wash over him. He hadn't expected such a request, but the more he thought about it, the more logical the idea became in his mind. If the Sioux children understood the modern language, and could both speak, write, and read English, they would have a better chance at dealing with all the changes the government might place on them.

"I've heard of Indian schools where the Cavalry come and take the Indian children from their families and force them into these acclimation schools to become more like settlers. I think this would be better for the children. If the Cavalry does come, they will see that the children are learning properly in a school environment already."

"That was our line of thinking as well. We might be a little remote town, but the news of what is going on in the country is still making its way here. Brown Bear wants to be prepared for anything," Mathew said as he exchanged a glance with his wife. Jenny gave him a smile before the couple focused back on Dan.

"When does Brown Bear want to meet?" Dan then asked.

"Whenever you have time. He's willing to meet when you're available," Mathew explained.

"Do you think you two would be able to join me? I've never been up to the camp before." Jenny smiled at Dan as she nodded.

"We always like an excuse to go to the camp. Mikey just loves playing with the other children, and Bailey has really taken to the wolf cub one of Brown Bear's warriors found on a hunt," Jenny said.

"How does Saturday sound for you?" Mathew asked.

"I can do Saturday. I don't have any lessons scheduled for this coming Saturday," Dan agreed. "Do I need to bring anything special?"

Mathew smiled as he said, "Nope. Just be yourself. We'll come pick you up in the wagon if you want?"

"Sure, I'd like that." Dan wasn't so sure about this meeting, but he liked the idea of having more students to teach and thought it would be a good challenge for him. But the more he thought about it, the more he realized the potential dangers of it too.

"I'm going to go see if I can catch the Mayor before he heads out for the day. If I'm going to be teaching Indian children here at the town hall, he should have a heads up," Dan explained then.

"That's a good idea," Mathew said as a look of concern crossed his face. He hadn't thought about the town's reaction to Dan teaching the Indian children. He had only thought about what a great benefit it would be. "I hope no one in town would oppose this idea."

"Well, that's why I'm going to go talk to the Mayor first thing. If he stands behind me then I won't have to worry what anyone else thinks," Dan said.

"We'll leave you to it, then," Jenny said as she let Mikey

back down on the floor to walk with her. "Thank you for at least being open to the idea."

"I see the benefit of it for the Indian tribe. It would be selfish of me to deny anyone an education if I can provide it to them, no matter who they are," Dan said as he walked with the Jenkins family to the front of the town hall. The Mayor's office was just at the opening of the building.

"That's what makes you the best schoolteacher," Jenny said with a smile. "You have a passion for teaching others and really care about your students." Dan couldn't contain his own smile at the compliment. He was speechless as he nodded to them as they left the town hall. It was always nice to be recognized for his profession.

Once Dan had collected himself, he knocked on the Mayor's door. He hollered for him to enter, and as Dan opened the door, he saw that the Mayor had papers all over his desk. For a moment Dan forgot about why he had knocked on the door in the first place as he stepped in and looked at all the organized chaos around him.

"Working on something big?" Dan asked as he looked around. The Mayor picked up a stack of papers on his desk and tapped them together on the wooden surface before adding them to another pile of straightened papers.

"Just doing some research for the town is all," Mr. Franklin replied with a kind smile. "What brings you in, Mr. Mavis?"

"Well, I just had a conversation with the Jenkins' family. Mathew and Jenny came in with their son, Mikey."

"Oh yeah? Trying to get their toddler into school a little early?" the Mayor asked with a chuckle.

"As cute as that would be, I don't think the other students would focus on their studies after that. They'd all be too determined to teach the young boy this and that," Dan said as he joined the Mayor in a bit of laughter. "No, Mathew came to talk to me about Brown Bear and the other Sioux Indians. The Chief would like the tribe's children to start attending lessons here at the town hall so that I might teach them to speak English, as well as read and write it to better prepare for the future."

The Mayor's jaw dropped open as he spoke. He looked at Dan with wide eyes as he thought about what the schoolteacher had just told him. This was certainly not something he'd ever considered before, and with all the other plans he was currently working on, he wondered how this might affect him.

"Well, what did you tell Mathew?"

"I agreed to at least meet with Brown Bear and discuss it with him. I don't mind teaching them English because I think it would be very beneficial for the children. No one knows what's going to happen next between the government and the Indians, and lately things aren't getting any better. Have you heard about the Cavalry stealing Indian children from their tribes and putting them into acclimation school?"

The Mayor nodded as a grim expression settled over his face. "Yes, I've heard about them. Not going to share my opinion on that matter. But if Brown Bear is willing to send the children to school, then I think that gives him a lot of credit. I think that's wise of him to decide that."

"My only other concern is what the town will think. Not everyone likes Indians, and I, myself, haven't spent much time around them. I'm not prejudiced, but I did ask the Jenkins to accompany me to the camp since it will be my first time going up there."

"I don't blame you. Even after what they did for the town, saving all those men and Rosa Casey from that deadly cough, I'm just not one hundred percent certain about the Sioux. This might be the thing that helps me understand them more, though."

"You have many valid points, Mr. Franklin. But if I knew that the Mayor supported this effort, then I would have more confidence when I go to meet Brown Bear this Saturday."

"As of right now, I see no issues with the Indian children learning English. Heck, some of the town's people who don't even like Indians might support that idea. As long as they don't start any trouble, or there are no issues with the other children, I will support this effort fully," the Mayor said as he stood from his desk. He came around and shook Dan's hand, reassuring the schoolteacher that this was the right thing to do.

"Thank you very much, Mr. Franklin. I'll let you know how it goes Saturday."

"Very good. Well, let's get out of here. Seems like I've done all I can for today."

Dan followed the Mayor out of the town hall and waited while he locked up the front doors. In the past, they hadn't worried about locking up the building because there weren't too many valuables inside. Plus, the townspeople were trustworthy and wouldn't steal from their own town hall. But after the bank robbery attempt in the past, the Mayor had started to take more precautions as of late.

Dan nodded to the Mayor before making his way over to the livery stables where he kept his gelding. He had a small cottage outside of town and wanted to get home in time to update his students records of how they were all progressing. As he rode out of town, he thought about the upcoming harvest as he looked out over the countryside, seeing field after field of hay, wheat, oats, and corn. Thanks to the local farmers, the town was able to have many things such as flour, oatmeal, and, of course, corn. It also provided the cattle ranches with feed for their herds.

Dan very much liked Bear Creek and the strong-knit community. Some people might not be able to handle the small-town gossip or always running into the same people time and time again. But it provided Dan with a sense of comfort knowing he could rely on his neighbors. He liked being such a help to everyone, especially when it came to teaching people the basic skills of reading and writing.

As Dan rode up to his cottage about a quarter of a mile from town, he led his gelding into the small stable beside the cottage, just big enough for two horses. There, he unsaddled his horse and made sure to brush him well before filling his feed bag and shutting the stall door. Dan then made his way into his cottage, the warm air from the day greeting him immediately. Dan chuckled, realizing he forgot to open up the shutters that morning to let all the hot air escape. He made quick work of the chore before scrounging up something to eat for dinner.

It was very normal for Dan to settle down in the main room at the small table with only two chairs with a plate of only cheese and bread. Dan was a very simple man in that he liked routine and more than likely the same meal over and over again. Because he was so busy with his lessons and planning in the evening, he needed the most minimalist way of providing for his needs. Therefore, his small cottage only consisted of one other room, his bedroom. In the main room was a modest kitchen with a dry sink and cooking stove, and in the center was a table where he prepared his lessons or made other documentations. He had very little décor with only donated curtains over the windows. There was a fireplace and chimney that he kept in the winter time, but there was no other furniture besides the table and chairs.

A part of Dan thought that there was simply no need for anything else. He had a bookcase in his bedroom that he used to store books that he couldn't at the town hall. There was a bed and dresser in his bedroom, enough to provide for his needs. A well was in the backyard so he could fetch water locally, and the outhouse was located about twenty steps from the back door. All in all, Dan had everything he needed and not much else.

The other half of Dan realized, however, that he didn't want to purchase anything else for the small cottage until he had a family of his own. Perhaps his wife would like to decorate the stone cottage or help him decide on other furniture. Maybe an addition would need to be added to the cottage to provide more space and room for children or relatives, if his wife came from a large family. His parents and siblings still lived in Texas, and therefore Dan rarely had the opportunity to go see them. They'd never made the trip up north to see him either.

His modest cottage was just another reminder of how badly Dan wanted a family of his own. He wanted someone to share this space with and turn it into their forever home. He wanted to hear the sound of laughing children echoing off these rounded walls, filling his memory of happy days and joy-filled moments. Till he had that family, Dan saw no need to do anything to the cottage. It had the bare minimum, and that satisfied him for the time being.

Dan's thoughts drifted away from the notes he was making on all the students reports he kept at home in a journal. He was thinking about the letters he had received today and how none of them had interested him. Dan knew that there was still a chance that he could meet a woman that shared his level of interest and intelligence. He only hoped that he would meet this woman sooner rather than later.

CHAPTER 3

*S*aturday came sooner than Dan had realized. After finishing out the week with his students and the private tutoring lessons, not to mention the book club meeting on Friday, Saturday snuck up on Dan. He'd been in his cottage, drying and putting away the dishes from breakfast when a knock was heard on his front door. He thought it was strange that he would receive a visitor at home because he saw most of the town's people on a regular basis during his teaching hours. But as he approached the front door to greet whoever had come to see him, it finally dawned on him what day it was.

"Good morning, Mathew," Dan said with a smile. He wasn't going to admit to his friend that he'd just forgotten about their arrangement. Instead, he put up the appearance that he was all ready to go. "I was just finishing up the dishes. Let me grab my saddle bag and I'll be ready to go. I figure a notebook and a graphite pencil will suffice for any notes."

"Way to think ahead," Mathew agreed. Dan left the front

door open as he went to quickly collect his things. Then, he followed Mathew out of the door with his leather saddle bag hung over his shoulder, ready as ever to meet with the Sioux Chief.

Out on the main road into town sat Jenny in the wagon with little Mikey on her lap. They sat in the back with the ever-obedient cattle dog, Bailey. Hay bales had been positioned so Jenny could sit comfortably without having to worry about being tossed around too much as the wagon was pulled by the two-horse team. Mathew pulled himself up onto the driver's bench, and Dan used the wagon wheel to sit on the other side next to him.

"Good morning, Dan. Ready to head to camp?" Jenny asked with a bright smile.

"Sure am. I've never been to an Indian camp before so I'm curious to know what it will be like," Dan replied. Mikey hung on to the hay bales with his hands and stood on his little legs, his blue eyes bright and shining in the morning sun. Bailey had become a protective dog since the little boy's birth and sat next to him, ready to spring into action if the child fell during the wagon ride.

"I can't wait to see your reaction when we make it to camp. It's something else when you see them all together for the first time," Mathew said with a chuckle. "The first time Brown Bear brought me to camp, I thought I was going to have a heart attack. I had no idea there were so many Indians living so close to all of us."

Dan simply smirked and nodded in response. He wasn't sure what to expect, but he was willing to go if it meant increasing the size of his class. The schoolteacher only had ten students and thought a larger class would not only be fulfilling, but he'd get to practice a different skill of teaching children a second language. He was up for the challenge, if only he could get over his fear of meeting all the Indians from the Sioux tribe at once.

Mathew steered the wagon through town before taking the only path wide enough for a wagon up into the hills and mountains that were just outside of the main town. Bear Creek had been founded around the mines and named after the bears that frequented the creek that ran down from the top of the mountain. Dan hadn't spent much time in the mountains, only hiking the round about hills to view the stunning sunsets in the evening. He tried to imagine he was going on a grand adventure like a hero from one of the novels he'd read in the past.

They disappeared into the forest as the wagon continued to travel higher and higher into the elevation. The worn path began to switch back and forth up the mountain. Dan looked out through the forest, feeling as though he'd been transported into a different world. Bird song filled the air as sunlight peeked down through the canopy. All manner of fauna and flora spread out in every direction, with squirrels chasing one another and tall grasses growing in the shade around trees. Dan was so lost in thought that at first he didn't hear Mathew's question.

"You alright there?" Mathew asked. Dan turned to his friend and smiled.

"Sorry. I was just getting carried away with the scenery. What did you say?"

"I asked if you heard about Margret and Louis Fritz?" Mathew restated.

"No. What about them?"

"They've started dating," Jenny answered from the back of the wagon. Dan looked over his shoulder at her as she smiled happily, holding onto Mikey with one hand as he tried to toddle around the wagon. Bailey kept moving his position, always trying to stay very close to the boy.

"Well, that sounds like a good thing. I know they are both older, but I think love is possible at any age," Dan reasoned.

"They've only been on a few dinner dates together, so it's hard to say if they have any strong feelings for one another yet," Mathew added. "But it's good to see Margret so blissfully happy in the evenings. Especially when she gets done cleaning the bank on Wednesdays." They all laughed at that as the trees started to thin. Dan looked ahead of them to see where the path was leading to, and as soon as the wagon passed through another tree line, Dan was completely amazed by what he saw.

As far as the eye could see, Dan saw Indians of all ages and genders walking around the camp. He spotted maidens weaving baskets or working at a loom to push strands of fabric together to form beautifully made wool blankets of intercut designs of red, white, and black. Warriors just back from the hunt carried their prized deer on a long pole between them. The moment they set it down, maidens joined them in skinning the animal to be used in all manner of ways.

All of it intrigued Dan because he'd never seen for himself how Indians lived. He'd read plenty of books, but this was the first time he honestly got to see an Indian village in action. Everyone had a job and was either preparing something, making a tool or item that was needed, or helping someone else. It was truly the highest level of community support a group of people could create. What was even more surprising was, as Mathew pulled the wagon to a halt, he spotted Edward and Phoebe James amongst the throng of Indians.

Dan was transfixed with the sight of them as he slowly got down from the wagon once Mathew put on the wheel brake. In a sea of deerskin maiden gowns and tunics and trousers on the warriors, Phoebe James stood out in her dark purple gown with long sleeves trimmed in white lace. Her long, dark brown hair was pulled back from her face in a simple design, causing it to cascade down her back in waves. Every time Dan saw Phoebe, he was always awestruck by her beauty.

"Ah, it looks like the James siblings are in camp," Mathew commented, seeing in which direction Dan was looking. He'd spotted him staring at something for almost a solid minute, and once he followed his friend's eyesight, he couldn't help but smile when he noticed the person that had captured his full attention.

Dan snapped back to reality as he looked at Mathew, composing himself once more. He nodded once before turning around to help Jenny and Mikey down from the back of the wagon. Bailey jumped down and started to sniff the ground. He then let out a happy bark and dashed across the camp in search of something.

"Looks like Bailey has gone in search of his friend," Jenny said with a chuckle. She held onto Mikey's hand and led him through camp. Dan followed closely behind the Jenkins as they neared the central fire. Many Indians sat around here, to include Brown Bear as he petted his wolf cub. Bailey came over to him and barked once. Brown Bear nodded to the cattle dog and allowed his wolf cub to go and play with the other dog. Dan couldn't help but think the scene before him was very traditional, like a parent giving another child permission to go play with one of his own.

"Greetings, friends," Brown Bear said as he spotted Mathew coming near with Jenny and Mikey. "It is always good to see you."

"It is good to see you, too, Brown Bear," Mathew replied as

they embraced, slapping each other on the back enthusiastically. "I have brought with me the schoolteacher from town."

Brown Bear stepped away from Mathew and peered past Jenny and the little one to spot the young man Mathew had told him about. The Indian chief observed him closely, noticing his tall height and lengthy body. He didn't appear anything like one of his warriors, but there was a deep wisdom that Brown Bear saw in his eyes as they both looked at each other.

"Welcome, schoolteacher. Thank you for coming all this way to speak with me," Brown Bear said to address the man.

"Thank you, Brown Bear. My name is Dan Mavis and I have been teaching in Bear Creek for the last five years," Dan said as he stepped closer to the towering Indian Chief. The man's eyes were like two dark obsidians that Dan felt he could fall into and never return. Though he smiled at Dan, there was something about the chief that radiated authority and power.

"Please, have a seat with me," Brown Bear suggested as he pointed to the space on the log beside him. Dan obliged the chief and took a seat on the log as he withdrew his notebook and graphite pencil, prepared to take any notes that he might need to remember from his conversation with Brown Bear.

"Now, I'm sure that Mathew has explained the reasoning behind this meeting," Brown Bear started with.

"Indeed. He explained that you are wanting the Indian children to attend the school lessons in order to learn English, as well as to read and write the language," Dan said as he flipped the notebook open to a blank page.

"That is correct. I believe the children would benefit from learning English in order to survive in the world that is quickly being formed around them. Only a few others and I know the White language. It has benefited me greatly as chief. I want my people to survive after I am gone. I have a strong feeling from the Great Spirit that the children of the tribe must learn English as soon as possible."

"I agree with you that there would be benefits for them when it comes to their entire lives. But how many children are you hoping to send to school?" Dan looked around the camp again, realizing that this was a large people. If every child were to attend the lessons, he wasn't sure if the town hall would be large enough or if one teacher would be enough to teach the lessons efficiently.

"To begin with, I would send ten of the brightest young ones that I believe would be able to learn the language quickly. Once they have learned, they'll be able to teach others in the tribe. Therefore, by teaching ten of them to speak, write, and read English, they will be able to teach ten students each themselves. Perhaps in a few short years, the entire tribe might know English well enough."

Dan raised his eyebrows at the statement, never having thought about this situation in that light. He'd never thought about his students one day teaching others. It really made Dan realize how important his role would be in ensuring an entire tribe of people learned a second language.

"Your goal is a very lofty one," Dan admitted. "Though I think it is a reasonable idea. It is uncertain what the government will decide next when it comes to the Indian tribes in the country. It would be beneficial to at least know the language if anything certainly does happen."

"Then it seems that we both see eye-to-eye on the matter. I shall send my chosen ten to the town hall on Monday. They can be there as early as the rising of the sun," Brown Bear explained.

"I normally make it to the town hall by the time the sun is already up. Many of my students have to travel into town for their lessons because most live on farms. An hour after sunrise will suffice," Dan reassured the chief.

"Then it shall be so. As this new arrangement begins, what are your worries and fears about teaching my children English?" Brown Bear asked. Dan thought this was a very good question to ask and he took a minute to gather his thoughts.

"From a teaching perspective, my biggest challenge will be communicating to the children you have chosen. It will take time for them to learn to trust me, and to also understand what I am trying to teach. I will start with easy things to learn to say, like 'hello' and 'how are you'. It will be basic for some time. Despite the challenge of the lessons, the other difficulty might come from the town's people themselves. Not everyone likes Indians, and though I don't think anyone would cause any trouble, the children might face some animosity simply for who they are."

Brown Bear nodded as he listened to Dan's explanation. These were the same things he had imagined might pose an issue.

"I've already talked to the Mayor and he has decided to support me with teaching the Indian children," Dan quickly added.

"This is good to hear," Brown Bear said. "I like the Mayor and am glad to hear the man will support this arrangement as well."

"There might be talk in town whether it is right or wrong for me to be teaching the Indian children. But I, at least, promise you that I won't allow any harm to come to them."

Brown Bear nodded and gave Dan a grunt, which the school-teacher wasn't sure about the meaning of. But as Brown Bear turned the conversation to the others sitting around the central fire, he figured he'd been dismissed. Standing, Dan repositioned himself on the other side of the fire pit to take notes. He only had a few things to document, but was glad to have developed a better idea as to why the Indian chief wanted a few number of children to learn English. It was an exciting idea to know that he would be a part of an entire Indian tribe learning English. He was eager to get started right away.

Dan's thoughts were interrupted as Phoebe James settled down on the log next to him. He was surprised by her presence and assumed that she was going to speak to him about the book they'd been reading with the club. Dan closed his notebook and turned his attention on Phoebe and was about to greet her when she spoke up first.

"Do you know how to speak Sioux?" she asked.

"I do not," Dan replied as he furrowed his brows. He wondered what the direct question would lead to.

"How do you expect to teach the Sioux children if you can't communicate with them?" Phoebe then asked. An idea immediately formed in Dan's head and he decided to take a risk and run with the thought.

"I have a few ideas. But do you speak the language?" Dan asked.

Phoebe nodded as she said, "My brother began to teach me when we were traveling to Bear Creek for the first time. He's part Sioux and spent some time with his mother learning the culture and the language. I've learned quite a lot since I spend most of my time up here in the mountains and prefer the Indian camp over the mines."

"In that case, I think you should join me for the lessons. You could be my interpreter and could surely teach the children English as well as I could. After all, you've had similar education to what I have, if only in a different setting," Dan suggested. He watched as Phoebe focused her large brown eyes on him, seeming to think about his offer. Dan's heartbeat raced as he tried to wait patiently for her response. He knew that it was a good idea to have some extra help with this special arrangement, but it also meant that he could spend some more quality time with the woman he was attracted to.

"I care about these children very much and think it would be wise if they had a familiar face in the classroom to look up to. I can communicate with them easy enough and describe your lessons to them in their own language," Phoebe agreed. "I think we could make this work."

"I'd appreciate all the help I can get. But I would insist that the Indian children speak as much English as possible when they are in the town hall. If they are to learn English quickly and proficiently, practice will make perfect. I don't want them to rely on you so much that they don't learn anything," Dan said, making sure Phoebe understood the basics of his plan to teach the children.

"I think I can handle that part," Phoebe said with a smile. "Why did you agree to teach the children English?" Dan hadn't been expecting this question, but figured it was reasonable enough to wonder why he would do this when he wasn't acquainted with the tribe at all.

"I honestly believe that anyone who is willing should receive the education they desire," Dan said after a moment of thought. "I do see the benefit for the Indian children to learn English. And after hearing Brown Bear's plan to have the entire tribe one day learn English, I think it would be wrong of me to deny an entire people the opportunity to develop."

Phoebe really looked at Dan Mavis then, taking in his appearance. He wasn't like the typical man she would have dated when she lived in Boston. Most of her suitors had been business owners that could provide a very comfortable life for Phoebe, as well as the opportunity to remain in the limelight of society. She'd been a debutante once and a very popular one at that.

Ever since coming to Bear Creek, with little choice in the matter, Phoebe had put off any idea of ever dating again. She'd live her life based on her own standards and support her cast-off brother in his endeavors. Phoebe spent most of her days either tending to their small cabin or being at the Indian camp to be around people who wouldn't judge her but instead welcome her with open arms and teach her all sorts of things she'd never dreamed of learning. She could make Indian jewelry now and other types of bead work.

Out of all the men that had tried to ask Phoebe out on a date, Dan Mavis hadn't been one of them. She enjoyed discussing literature with him during the book club meetings, and sometimes she wondered just how far his intelligence went. She, as well as anyone else, could tell that Dan was a very caring person. He cared deeply for his students, both young and old, and always went out of his way to make sure all the members of the book club were comfortable when they all came together. And though Phoebe suspected that Dan might have feelings for her, he'd never acted on those feelings as of yet.

Phoebe was very impressed with Dan and his willingness to teach the Indian children English. Phoebe had already been thinking about the possible challenges of this task when she first heard of the idea circulating amongst the Indian maidens. Some of the tribe members agreed with the idea that learning English would be a large benefit for the tribe as a whole. But many mothers didn't like the idea of sending their children to the town each day for lessons. They felt that a few braves should go with them to make sure they were protected.

With the idea of accompanying the children each day to their lessons, Phoebe was certain she could comfort many of these mothers and their concerns. She would not only make sure they were safe, but she'd be a familiar face in the classroom that they could turn to if they were experiencing any issues.

"I think what you are doing is both a good thing and a brave thing," Phoebe said as she looked away from Dan, seeming to finally break through from her deep thought process. "I can only imagine how many people from town will oppose the idea and try to make trouble for you."

"I only like to deal with problems when they arise," Dan said. "Till then, I won't waste time speculating on the ifs and maybes of a situation. It might distract me from tackling the real problem at hand." Phoebe was surprised to hear this line of thinking. It really demonstrated what a deep thinker Dan Mavis was and how he could actually keep up with her if they were to have a long conversation together about unconventional things.

"Well, I should go let Brown Bear know I will be accompanying the children to town and be there during their English lessons. I don't think he would oppose it, but he should know none the less," Phoebe said as she rose from the log.

"I look forward to having your assistance," Dan said as he stood with her. "I'll see you Monday morning."

Phoebe left him with a nod and a small smile before rounding the central fire and making her way over to Brown Bear. She was swimming in a sea of thoughts as she walked, reflecting on Dan and his pure intentions and also the task she'd signed herself up for. Phoebe enjoyed working with the children and thought this task of helping them to learn English would give her life purpose. After all, if she'd given up the idea of marriage then at least she should find something to occupy all her time with.

Dan stood for a few seconds, simply watching Phoebe walk away from him. When he'd agreed to help teach the Indian children, he would have never thought he'd get a chance to spend more time with the woman he often thought about. He settled back down on his log and opened his notebook, tuning out everyone around him as he started to lesson plan. But every once in a while his thoughts would return to Phoebe, causing a smile to appear on his face at the idea of getting to work with her every day of the week.

CHAPTER 4

hoebe rose early Monday morning, well before the rising of the sun. She'd even beaten her brother by waking first and beginning to get ready for the day. Normally it was her brother that woke before the crack of dawn to prepare another descent into the mines to oversee the work for the day. Currently, he had a good crew on his hands and was working with the miners he'd hired. Phoebe was certain that the good work ethic had something to do with the living conditions the miners were given. Mr. and Mrs. Tibet who owned the inn in town had also purchased the boarding house when the former owner passed away. With the Mayor's help, the boarding house was restored to a finer living arrangement, bringing in the best quality of workers.

Phoebe mused that things were really turning out for her brother as she finished dressing by candlelight and began to fix her hair back into a simple braid. If she'd been in Boston still, she'd have slept till the sun was already before the horizon and would have relied on her lady's maid to help her ready for the day. She'd never tried doing her own hair till she was on the train with Edward heading west. After a few years, she'd gotten used to doing things for herself that she'd grown up used to someone else doing for her. A lot had changed, but she wouldn't trade it for the world. Especially after everything that had happened right before she fled Boston with her half-brother.

Stepping out into the main room of the cabin, Phoebe took with her the candle she'd lit earlier and used it to light a few lanterns around the room to shed light on the dark space. Hues of orange were flowing in through the windowpanes as the sun started to rise. She made quick work of fixing a light breakfast of bacon and eggs so that she and Edward would have something on their stomachs before starting any hard work. It must have been the smell of food that woke Edward and coaxed him out of his room because he stepped into the main room in only his long johns.

"You're quite indecent," Phoebe mused as she flipped the bacon and cracked two eggs into the hot skillet, the sound of sizzling eggs filling the room.

"Why on earth are you up so early?" he asked as he scratched his head and yawned.

"I've volunteered to escort the Indian children who are taking English lessons to town. I will remain with them and help to translate Mr. Mavis' lessons. In the afternoon, I shall return with them," Phoebe explained without taking her eyes off the food she was preparing.

"You're going to help teach them English?" Edward asked as he fetched two tin cups down from the cupboard and set them on the table. He then fetched the kettle and dipped it into the bucket of water he'd fetched the night before so he could fix them both a cup of coffee.

"I don't have much of anything else to do. It will make it

easier on the children if they know someone in the classroom, and since I know the language, I can help translate," Phoebe continued. She then slid the food she'd prepared onto two wooden plates. It was another reminder of what Phoebe had given up by coming out west. She'd grown up dining on porcelain plates, something she hadn't seen since leaving Boston.

"Well, that's mighty kind of you," Edward said as he set the kettle on the stove. "Guess I better go get dressed." Phoebe chuckled as she looked over her shoulder and watched her brother disappear into his room. Indian braves often spent the summer in nothing but a breechcloth, so Phoebe was used to the sight of bare flesh on a man. It also caused her to remember a memory she still tried very hard to push down. Phoebe set about washing the skillet while the breakfast cooled, hoping to also wash away the terrible memories.

When Edward returned in his work clothes, they sat down at the table together with a fresh cup of coffee and a decent breakfast. They ate quickly without conversation, both of them needing to be somewhere that morning.

"Just be safe while you're out there. I know you'll be fine, but I wouldn't be able to keep my head focused if I didn't tell you as much before leaving for the day," Edward said as he pulled on his miner's hat to protect his brown hair from all the dirt and dust of the mines.

"Go on with you now," Phoebe said with a chuckle. "I shall tell you all about my adventures with the children this evening."

"Good luck then," Edward said before he picked up his pickaxe from beside the door and pulled on his dirty boots. He opened the door and closed it again, leaving Phoebe to quickly clean up after their breakfast and finish gathering her things for the day. She wasn't sure what all she would need, so she brought some extra sheets of writing paper and a few graphite pencils she had for when she liked to sketch different things in the forest. She figured the Indian children could use them for when they started practicing writing their letters.

Phoebe left the modest cabin and made her way to the stables. Here, the miners kept their horses during the day when they were in the mines. Phoebe saddled her mare after giving her a good breakfast, and as she pulled herself onto the saddle, she carefully led the horse from the stable and towards the trail that would take her to camp.

Learning to ride a horse was another thing that had been new to Phoebe when she'd moved from a big city to practically the middle of nowhere. Without her father's carriage to take her to all the places she wanted to go, Phoebe had to either walk the entire distance or learn to ride a horse. After her first few trips to the Indian camp with Edward on foot, Phoebe had decided to let the other Indian maidens teach her how to ride one of their ponies. Riding bareback had been rather uncomfortable because she didn't wear the same garb as the maidens, who wore long gowns made of deerskin and trousers made from the same material. In her long gown and petticoats, Phoebe had been forced to not only learn to ride in a saddle, but side-saddle at that. Phoebe knew that even though she might live in the country now, she wasn't going to give up her ideals of being a proper lady.

Therefore, after months of practice, Phoebe could now ride easily from the stables to the Indian camp with her side-saddle. With the rising sun, Phoebe watched the forest come to life around her. It was the main thing that Phoebe loved about living high in the mountains. The forest was always brimming with life, and as morning began, she was able to spot many forest creatures rising and getting to their own work of scavenging or chasing one another around. In the distance, Phoebe spotted a small grouping of deer. If the Indian warriors were out that morning, they would surely spot them. Phoebe loved to see this wildlife around her as she slowly made her way to camp.

As the tree line thinned and gave way, she crossed into the clearing where the Sioux Indians kept their camp. From what she'd learned from this people, their families had lived in this spot for over ten generations. In the winter, the tribe would move south for warmer weather and better hunting opportunities. But with the rising oppression from the settler's government, this people had chosen to remain hidden up in the mountains.

Phoebe pulled her mare to a halt in front of the small group of children that had been gathered by their mothers to prepare for the journey into town. She looked at them, five girls and five boys of about nine and ten years of age. Phoebe remembered starting her tutoring lessons when she was only five and thought the children weren't quite that old to have missed any serious learning opportunities. It would take time, she was sure, but it wouldn't be an impossible task to teach them the English language.

"It seems we are all ready," Phoebe spoke to them in their native language. The children looked up at her on the horse, all looking apprehensive.

"You will look after our children well?" asked one of the mothers as she stepped closer to her horse.

"Yes, Singing Water, I shall watch over the children. I will be with them continually and make sure they come to no harm," Phoebe replied in a strong tone. She didn't want her voice to betray her when she was feeling a bit nervous herself.

"What weapon do you carry with you to offer them protection?" Singing Water retorted, looking at Phoebe's legs and arms for any signs of a dagger.

"I don't need to carry weapons. I have the keen ability to always win an argument, especially with men," Phoebe replied, causing the children to chuckle along with a few of the mothers. But Singing Water didn't look convinced.

"If anything happens to my son, I will blame you," Singing Water said as she pointed a finger at Phoebe. She then turned and quickly walked off, her shoulders tense. Phoebe frowned, feeling like she could have said something else to comfort the woman. But it seemed that unless she proved herself, there would be no other way to convince the Indian mothers that their children were safe with her.

"Mount your ponies, children. Let us be off to town for the daily lessons. Make sure you have something for lunch," Phoebe instructed as she turned her focus back on the children. The mothers helped the children mount the four ponies that had been lent to the children for the purpose of traveling to and from town. They all held buckskin pouches around their shoulders that would no doubt contain meat jerky or maize patties. It would be enough to fill their stomachs till they returned that afternoon.

At the front, Phoebe led the small group down the mountain along the trail that led to the town below from the Indian camp. The farther they traveled from the Indian camp, the more the children began to chatter. Phoebe couldn't help but smile as she joined in with their conversations.

"What is it like to go to school with the White people?" Grasshopper asked, one of the youngest in the group.

"There is a large building in town called a town hall. There, Mr. Mavis teaches the other children in the community. We shall all go there and you will learn to speak English. I will help you," Phoebe simply explained.

"But won't the town's people chase us out because we are Sioux?" came Squirrel's question next. She was one of the older girls in the group and Phoebe could see the true concern on the girl's face.

"No, they will not chase us away. The Mayor of the town has already agreed to this arrangement. And I have made a very big promise to your mothers that I will not let any harm come to you all. That is a promise I plan to keep," Phoebe said sternly. The children all focused their eyes on her for a moment and Phoebe wasn't about to break underneath their many stares.

"Mr. Mavis is a very kind man. He looks forward to teaching you English. I believe you will all enjoy your lessons each day," Phoebe said, hoping to fill them with excitement instead of fear. "And if you all do good in your lessons, I shall buy you all a piece of candy from the general store." This caused the children to cry out in excitement because getting candy from the town was a very rare treat indeed. Phoebe couldn't help but smile brightly at all of their excitement. She really wanted these children to enjoy their lessons and one day teach their tribe the language of the settlers.

DAN WAS STANDING on the front steps of the town hall, eager to greet his students on that fine Monday morning. He'd risen a bit earlier, made sure to put on some of his nicer teaching clothes, and took the time to comb his hair to the side in the latest fashion. He'd even eaten a decent breakfast and remembered to bring his notebook with him to town. Dan was looking forward to starting the new lessons with the Indian children. And a part of him was even more excited to be seeing Phoebe James once again.

As his regular students started coming into town, having either been dropped off by parents who'd driven the wagon in that morning or siblings riding together on a horse, he greeted each one of them and instructed the students to find their places in the pews and begin practicing their words from last week on their slate tablets. About the time all his regular students had made it into their seats, Phoebe was seen leading a small group of Indian children through town.

Dan was mesmerized by her appearance, much like anytime he'd ever seen Phoebe. She'd dressed in a simple yellow day gown and had braided her long brown hair down her back. But it was the way that she held herself while riding side-saddle that really spoke to Dan. His eyes glanced at the four Indian ponies trailing behind her. The Indian children were all looking around with wide eyes, some of them simply curious while others looked afraid. But it was Phoebe who looked ahead and didn't pay attention to who was watching them or what their expressions were. Dan took the time to look around and did notice how some of the town's people had stopped in their goings to watch what was happening and it made Dan nervous if some sort of trouble would be started on the very first day of school for these children.

Once Phoebe reached the town hall, she dismounted and tied her horse to the hitching post. She then helped the Indian children down from their ponies and tied leads around the ponies to the hitching post so they wouldn't wander. Then, she instructed the children to follow her as she took the steps up to the front door of the town hall where Dan waited for them.

"Good morning, Mr. Mavis," Phoebe said in a cheerful voice. "May I introduce you to Brown Bear's chosen few." Phoebe said their names for Dan and he had a hard time realizing who was who. He figured that in time he'd learn all their names and for now was simply eager to meet them.

"Good morning, children," Dan said to the Indian group. The children simply looked back at him with curious eyes. Phoebe repeated Dan's greeting in Sioux and the children replied in their native tongue.

"Hou," or "Hau" they said, whether they were a young boy or girl.

"You should greet Mr. Mavis by saying 'Hello'," Phoebe instructed to the children. They all looked at her and then back at the schoolteacher before trying out the new word. As they all said hello to Dan, he smiled at them and said hello back.

"Let's head inside and greet the other children. I'm sure they are eager to meet you as well," Dan said as he waved them all in. Phoebe translated for him and together they entered the town hall. Dan pointed to the pews and the Indian children sat down in them, their eyes turning to the other students in the room.

"Children, today is the beginning of a grand arrangement between myself and Brown Bear, leader of the Sioux Indians," Dan said as he addressed his normal students. They were staring wide-eyed at the Indian children, probably never having seen an Indian up close before. "I have been given the task to teach them English. They will be joining us each day for our lessons. I like to think we could all be good teachers to them to help them learn English and to show them they have nothing to fear." Phoebe spoke quietly to the Indian children, translating for Dan.

"They have nothing to fear? What about us? Aren't they savages?" came Gravis Miller's voice, a thirteen-year-old boy who only came to town because his mother made him, thinking an education would help the boy in the long run.

"Gravis, I will hear no such talk come from your lips while you're in this building. And that's the same for the rest of you," Dan said in a stern voice as he looked into the eyes of every child, even the Indian ones. "I expect you all to respect one another because you are all human beings here to learn and better yourselves. God loves the Indians just as much as He loves each one of you. I won't say no to anyone wanting to learn English and better themselves."

The children looked at their schoolteacher, surprised by his words. Though Mr. Mavis could be hard on them sometimes when it came to learning, he'd never spoken to them in that type of tone before. They all understood that he was very serious. Even Gravis thought it was best to sit back down and quiet himself. Though, he was certain his parents wouldn't be thrilled once they learned that the schoolteacher was allowing Indian children to attend lessons.

Phoebe spoke quietly to the Indian children in their native tongue while Mr. Mavis spoke. She was proud to repeat his strong words in their native language so the Indian children could understand how serious the schoolteacher was when it came to their lessons. Phoebe wanted the Indian children to trust Mr. Mavis and really take their lessons seriously because it would mean a lot to their people one day.

As the morning progressed, Dan set up all the children with their daily lessons. He was experienced in teaching children of different ages and therefore had the skills to manage an entire room full of children as they all worked on different tasks. As he focused on working with all the Indian children, with Phoebe's help, they showed them how to use a slate tablet and chalk and how to practice writing the English alphabet with Phoebe repeating the name and sound of each letter. Phoebe explained to them in their language that these symbols represented individual letters, that when put together they would form English words. When they learned the name and sound of each letter, they would be able to sound out words in English.

The Indian children took their lessons very seriously, much like learning any other lesson from their elders. They understood how important it was that they learn English so that one day they could teach others in their tribe. But a few of the children wanted to show the other students in the room that they were both capable of learning English, and, perhaps, also being the best student in the entire class.

When the time came for the students to take a break and enjoy playing in the yard behind the town hall, Dan was a little worried about how the students would play together. He certainly wanted everyone to play along together, but with both the language barrier and other prejudiced ideas in their minds, Dan figured that if trouble was going to happen today, it would be during their play time.

"Alright, students. Let's take a break and stretch our arms and legs for a bit," Dan said as he stood at the front of the town hall. The sound of slates being tucked away underneath pews was heard as the children excitedly prepared for the break. They scattered from the pews and made their way out the back door in a hurry as Phoebe explained to the Indian children what was happening as they watched the other children run from the building in a hurry. Singing Water had been afraid that something terrible was happening, but when Phoebe explained they could go outside and play for a bit, she was curious to what games the other children played.

Phoebe led the Indian children out of the town hall and into the back yard. The day had warmed up with barely a cloud in the sky. A warm breeze swept across the land, sending scents of wildflowers into the air. Dan followed after them as well, eager to see how everyone would play together.

For a few minutes, the Indian children stood together close to Phoebe and watched the other children running around for a game of tag. Grasshopper watched the children, thinking the game looked like a lot of fun. He loved to run and tag others and thought he would try his luck. He ran from his friend's side and joined the other kids, tagging those around him as though he was the one who could tag the most people in the least amount of time. But when the regular students realized that one of the Indians had joined in on their game, they all stopped and stared at Grasshopper. The Indian boy stopped as well and was concerned with all eyes on him.

Dan was just about to walk up to the group to make sure no one picked on the young Indian boy when Phoebe grabbed his arm and pulled him to a stop. He turned and looked at her, not wanting to waste time in case trouble was about to begin.

"Wait and see what they do first," Phoebe suggested. "Let's not jump to conclusions just yet." Dan became very aware of Phoebe's hands on his arm and colored a bit at her warm touch. He nodded and turned away from her as she dropped her hands from him. He watched the group of children, waiting to see what would happen.

"Hello," Grasshopper said as he raised his right hand in greeting. The other children all looked at the Indian boy and at each other, wondering what they should do.

"No Indians allowed in our games," came Gravis' stern voice. Dan's heart dropped upon hearing the older boy's words.

"Oh, come on, Gravis. You're just upset because the Indian boy can run faster than you can," said Penelope, who was a year or two younger than Gravis. Her comment caused the other children to laugh, and as Grasshopper saw that these children were laughing, he smiled as well. Gravis just rolled his eyes as he quickly tagged Penelope and the game continued. Grasshopper joined in once more, tagging those around him as they tried hard to teach the boy how to actually play the game. After a while, the other Indian children joined in and soon all the children were running around laughing and playing, enjoying a game of tag and forgetting that they were honestly that different.

"It's a miracle," Dan said in a soft voice as he stood next to Phoebe. They were both watching the children intently, being constantly at the ready in case they would need to step between anyone.

"Parents place such high expectations on their children from such a young age that sometimes we forget that they are just children," Phoebe said. Dan turned his watchful eyes from the children and looked down at Phoebe. He wondered where that comment stemmed from and what in her past had caused such an opinion.

"Do you ever wish to have children?" Dan asked. Phoebe looked quickly at him, her brows furrowed. He immediately felt like he'd overstepped his boundaries with her and looked away. "You don't have to answer that question."

"I suppose I never really thought about it that much," Phoebe answered as she turned her eyes back on the children. They continued to chase after one another, the sound of their laughter filling the air. Even with the major differences between the students, their laughter all sounded the same.

"What about you? You teach children all day. Do you want any of your own?"

As Dan turned his head to gage her expression, he saw that a smirk lay upon her luscious lips and that it appeared that she took no offense to his question.

"I would like children of my own one day," Dan admitted. "I don't know how many I'd like or if I prefer a boy or girl. I simply know that after years of teaching, I'd like to feel that pride I see in other parents of seeing their children learn and grow."

Phoebe's face relaxed into almost a frown as she looked away from him again. He was dying to know what she was thinking, to understand her emotions and why she was reacting to his words in this particular way. It was like reading a mystery novel. Once the first few pages pulled you in, you didn't want to stop reading till you discovered all the book's secrets. He was starting to feel the same way towards Phoebe James.

After a little while longer, Dan called all the children back into the town hall with Phoebe's help as she talked to the Indian children. All the students had smiles on their faces as they came back inside for the afternoon lessons, chatting happily about how well they'd done in the game. Dan was just pleased to see that no one was fighting and that despite their differences, everyone could play together.

CHAPTER 5

The rest of the week passed in quite the same manner as Monday. Dan would rise early, be ready to greet all the students, and welcome the Indian children warmly when they arrived shortly after the majority of the students. Dan knew that they had the longest journey in the morning to reach the town hall and therefore couldn't be too hard on them when they sometimes ran a little late.

Dan was certainly impressed by the work ethic of the Indian children. They all tried very hard to learn the new English words by also memorizing the alphabet while trying to practice writing it. In a week, they were able to greet him at the door and ask simple questions such as, "How are you?" and give a reply when asked the same questions.

Furthermore, Dan was impressed by the way Phoebe interacted with all the children. Though she was primarily there to help the Indian children, she soon took a liking to all the students and was willing to help anyone who needed the help. It showed that Phoebe was not only educated, but she had a kind heart. It wasn't every young lady who'd be willing to help out with educational lessons, or to even help a different people learn a second language. Every day, Dan became more and more attracted to Phoebe James despite himself.

All seemed to be going well until Friday morning when the students started to arrive from out of town for their lessons. Gravis Miller usually rode to town on his own horse, but as Dan stood on the front steps of the town hall, he noticed Gravis riding into town with his father in the wagon. At first, Dan assumed that Mr. Miller had business in town, but when he stopped the wagon and they both got out, Dan knew that he needed to prepare himself for a confrontation.

"Good morning, Mr. Miller," Dan greeted as the man walked up the front steps with his son. Gravis nodded towards Dan before slipping in through the doors, appearing to be either afraid or guilty.

"Mr. Mavis, I hear that you're letting little redskin children in for school lessons," Mr. Miller said as he crossed his arms over his chest and peered down at Dan, for the man was a few inches taller than him.

"I am teaching the Indian children from the local Sioux tribe, yes. They are learning to speak English, as well as read and write the language," Dan informed him. He wasn't intimidated easily and wouldn't tolerate anyone's prejudice. This was something Dan knew would eventually happen, and in his idle time he'd mentally prepared his words for when a parent or another town's person approached him with this subject.

"Don't you think that's a little dangerous, letting trained fighters into the town hall? What if they turn on the other children?" Mr. Miller pressed.

"All the children have been working together very nicely this week. You should see them during the break, how they all laugh and play together. What you fail to see, Mr. Miller, is that they are all children, eager to learn and better themselves."

Mr. Miller looked down at Dan and narrowed his eyes. The schoolteacher waited for the parent to say something, but after a few more minutes, the man turned and stomped back down the stairs towards his wagon. The tension in Mr. Miller's shoulders told him that the man wasn't pleased with the situation. But regardless about how certain people felt about him teaching the Indian children English, he was going to keep on doing what he knew to be the right decision.

Thankfully by the time Mr. Miller had turned his wagon around and was making his way out of town, Phoebe and the Indian children were just coming into town from the north. He took a deep breath and pushed Mr. Miller's words out of his mind as he greeted them all warmly. The Indian children happily went inside, giving Dan a moment to talk to Phoebe.

"We had our first disapproving parent this morning," Dan said in a hushed tone. Phoebe looked concerned as she stopped at the back of the town hall with him. They were standing outside the Mayor's office and Dan wondered if he should report the situation to Mr. Franklin.

"I'm guessing it was Gravis' father," Phoebe said as she looked at the older boy at the front, seeing that the normally chatty boy was sitting very quietly.

"Indeed, it was," Dan said as he looked at the boy. He wasn't sure what type of conversation Gravis had with his parents, but by the way he was acting now, he could tell it wasn't a good one. "Mr. Miller isn't happy about the Indian children attending the school lessons with the other children. But this was to be expected. Unless the Mayor or the Sheriff tell me to stop what I'm doing, I'm not going to let a prejudiced parent stop me."

"You are very brave, Mr. Mavis. I don't think many schoolteachers would be willing to risk so much to teach Indians. I'm sure this is only the beginning of people voicing their tainted opinions," Phoebe commented.

Dan thought it was rather nice that Phoebe had complimented him. It was reassuring that he had Miss James' support, but that she also thought he was brave for doing what he only felt was right.

"Well, then. Let's get on with the day's lessons." Dan gave Phoebe a kind smile before making his way to the front of the town hall to address the students.

As he walked away, Phoebe slowed her pace in order to observe him closely. He wasn't very muscular, but instead was fit and trim. He was unlike most of the men she spent her time around, whether that was Edward and the miners or the Indian braves at the camp. Dan was unique in his own way but dedicated to his work and very intellectual. She was looking forward to the book club this afternoon after she took the Indian children back to the camp. She always thought it was interesting to hear Mr. Mavis' perspective on the section they'd all just read. The more time Phoebe was able to spend with the schoolteacher, the more interested she became in the man.

Get ahold of yourself, Phoebe silently scolded herself as she came to the front and began to explain to the Indian children in Sioux their instructions for the morning. She focused on the children, trying to rid her mind of any interesting thoughts concerning the schoolteacher. After all, she was here to do a service to Brown Bear and his people. This was a continued effort to find good terms between her brother and the Indian chief. But the more she spent helping the children and being around Dan, the more she realized how much she was really enjoying herself.

Ever since Dan had asked her the question about whether or

not she wanted any children of her own, she'd actually been thinking about it more and more. When she'd lived in Boston, the only concern she had was marrying well and living a life similar to the one she'd been born into. Her life was only designed for her to marry a wealthy man and live happily the rest of her life. But as she began to be courted by suitors, she began to gain a glimpse at what married life would really be like for herself. She'd be trapped underneath the ruling thumb of her husband and never be able to have such freedoms as she did with her parents. Any thought of having children of her own evaded her with such an opinion of marriage.

Though she'd learned much about marriage since coming to Bear Creek, especially amongst the Indians, she still hadn't thought much about her own marriage and future. She still didn't like the idea of being tied down by her husband or forced to do anything she didn't want simply because she was a married female and subject to her husband.

Phoebe tried hard to push those negative thoughts out of her mind as she worked with the students. This was no time to be contemplating such things when it mattered very little in the present time. But every time she glanced at Dan Mavis, she couldn't help but think of what type of husband he'd possibly make.

He wasn't sure what was going on today, but Dan had been catching Phoebe looking at him more often that day than what was normal. Usually she was either waiting for his next instructions or translating what he was trying to teach from English to Sioux. They worked well together and spent plenty of time working together with the children. But in the moments that the children were working individually on either a math problem or practicing their writing skills, Dan would look over at Phoebe as he often did to catch a glimpse of her to only find out that she was watching him all along. Sometimes she would turn her head quickly to appear as though she hadn't been watching him, and other times she would just smile or ask a clarifying question.

As they sat together outside as the children either played or ate their lunch, Dan thought it was finally time that he gathered up his courage to ask the question he'd wanted to ask Phoebe ever since the day he'd met her. He'd thought about it a lot and figured there would be a benefit for both of them if she agreed to his question.

"I've been thinking that if the Indian children are working hard at learning English that it would be decent of me to learn at least a little bit of Sioux," Dan said between bites of his own sandwich. "I was hoping you'd consider tutoring me on their language every once in a while."

Phoebe finished chewing her food before answering, giving her a moment to think about what she wanted to say. She'd been thinking about so much that day that she was surprised by the logical request.

"I can see why you'd want to learn some Sioux. It would be easier for you to communicate with the children," Phoebe reasoned.

"Or perhaps understand what they are saying or whispering when they don't think I can hear them," Dan explained with a chuckle. "I want them to speak as much English as possible when they are in town. But I think it would be beneficial for me to be able to understand them in return."

"When would you like to learn?" Phoebe asked. She knew that Dan had a very busy schedule between his lessons, tutoring, and the book club.

"Saturdays and Sundays I usually don't have things sched-uled unless Pastor Munster is in town and I can attend one of his sermons. Would you care to join me for dinner this Saturday night at the inn? We could practice while we eat." Dan's heart was beating fast in his chest as he waited for Phoebe's reply. She'd looked away from him, seeming to contemplate his words better.

"You would learn easier and faster if you came to the Indian camp and spent time there. You'd be surrounded by the language and, in turn, I could teach you what everyone is saying, much like I do for the children," Phoebe suggested. Though Dan was asking her to teach him Sioux, his request sounded more like asking her out on a date. She wasn't sure if she was ready for that type of thing, even after two years of being in Bear Creek.

Dan nodded, knowing that what Phoebe had suggested was the most reasonable thing to do. He was glad that at least Phoebe had agreed to teach him, but he was hoping to spend more time alone with her instead of constantly surrounded by people. He was hoping dinner would have been a good outlet. And though he truly did want to learn some Sioux, he also wanted to try his luck with Phoebe.

"It's been a long time since I've eaten at the inn, and I know that Mrs. Tibet and Mrs. Benning are wonderful cooks. I think I'd enjoy attending dinner with you there on Saturday to go over a few basic words," Phoebe said with a smile. She could see the rejected expression on Dan's face, a very similar expression to what most men looked like after she'd turned them down. But seeing it on Dan didn't settle well with her for whatever reason. Perhaps it was because she knew that Dan was a good man and that she never wanted to see him disappointed.

Dan tried to contain his glee as he looked at Phoebe and smiled. He could hardly believe his ears that she'd agreed to have dinner with him.

"How does six o'clock sound?" he asked.

"That would be fine."

With the matter out of the way, the two finished eating their lunch before gathering the children for the afternoon lessons. As Dan went about his day, all he could think about was his upcoming date with Phoebe. He tried to focus on the lessons, but he found himself losing his train of thought, causing the children to snicker from time to time. He'd just laugh right with them and continue on with their lessons.

By the time the school day was over, Dan felt like he had regained much of his composure. He bid all the students farewell as he walked with them out of the schoolhouse. And much to Dan's surprise, Mr. Miller had returned with a few of the other fathers, causing several of the school children to stop suddenly as they left the town hall. They appeared equally as surprised to see their fathers.

Phoebe came happily out of the town hall, speaking with the Indian children, telling them that there would be no more lessons till Monday. But she stopped suddenly, raising her hand up to stop the children behind her as she looked from Dan to the small group of men standing outside the town hall.

"What can I help you with, gentlemen?" Dan asked the group of five men.

"We don't think it's right what you're doing, Mr. Mavis," Mr. Miller spoke up first. Dan watched as Gravis went to go stand by his father, his face turned down as though he was ashamed of what was happening. It made Dan's heart drop that the children were getting to see such a spectacle of prejudice.

"I'm teaching children school lessons, like I always have," Dan replied as he took a step down from the town hall and neared the group. "I am doing nothing wrong and have continued to do what my profession calls for. I teach children without regards to their family name, status in the community, or their poverty." Dan was quick to make clear points regarding each of the men he was currently facing. They gave each other glances, knowing that they couldn't argue with that.

"It's not right to teach redskins English," came the voice of another father.

"And why is that?" Dan asked. "Because I see nothing wrong with a human being doing something to better themselves, to create a better future by seeking out a little bit of help. I know for certain that each one of you relies on the other to make sure your farms and cattle ranches stay profitable. After what the Indians have done for this town, in saving lives when even Dr. Harvey didn't have that knowledge, I see nothing wrong with returning that favor."

"Indians are dangerous people, Mr. Mavis. We just don't want to see our children hurt," came the voice of a third father. Dan looked at him, causing the man to look away.

"And I don't want to see these Indian children hurt because they're constantly surrounded by prejudiced people who think ill of them for no good reason. Your children are happy and safe during my lessons and thoroughly enjoy playing with the Indian children during our lunch break. Instead of judging me and those children up there, how about you first talk to your own children about what they are experiencing," Dan said, his temper starting to rise.

"Gravis here has been telling me plenty," Mr. Miller said with a snarl on his lips. "And he says he doesn't feel comfortable with those redskins."

Dan shifted his eyes down towards Gravis and saw how the boy watched his feet. Dan could tell that the boy felt guilty for what he had said, and maybe even guilty for what was happening now.

"Gravis is a wonderful student and a great friend to all the other children. And that includes the Indian children. Just today, young Singing Water fell while the children were playing and it was Gravis who came to her rescue and made sure she was alright. Despite him being uncomfortable, he's still been a great role model to the other children when it comes to everyone playing together."

Dan stared at all the men one by one to really place emphasis on what he was trying to say. Some would meet his gaze while others looked away.

"Be like Gravis. Even though you all might be uncomfortable with the idea, doesn't mean you should be unkind," Dan said in parting.

He then turned towards Phoebe as she stood in the doorway of the town hall, waiting to see what would happen. He motioned for her to come forward, making Phoebe feel proud to be working alongside a man who was willing to stand up for what he believed in. And the wit he had used to outsmart the men made Phoebe think that Dan was the perfect one to be teaching the Indian children English. That he would truly stand up for them.

Phoebe led the Indian children from the town hall after telling them to be brave. They came forthwith and nodded to the gentlemen before mounting their ponies. Phoebe pulled herself up onto her horse and gave the gentlemen a hard stare before turning her horse and leading the children out of town. She was feeling brave and proud of what she and Dan were able to accomplish. It was clear that neither one of them was going to back down when trouble came looking for them and the Indian children.

As Phoebe led the Indian children out of town, the fathers that had come to speak with Dan eventually turned away from the town hall and took their children home as well. Dan waited at the town hall for a while, making sure no one else was planning on coming to him and trying to sway his mind about who he was teaching. With everything seeming to settle down, Dan went inside and started to tidy up the town hall in preparation for the book club meeting that would happen in a little bit.

"That was some speech you gave out there," came a voice from the entrance of the town hall. Dan looked up from the notes he was making on each student and their progress and couldn't help but smile as he spotted Sheriff Benning coming his way.

"I didn't know I had an audience," Dan said with a smile. Though it did feel good to know that the Sheriff had seen him stand up for what he believed in.

"I had just come around the corner on the way to visit Rosa at work when I saw what was happening and came a bit closer just in case things got out of hand. Didn't know you were teaching Indian children now," the Sheriff admitted.

"Just started to this week. Brown Bear asked me to teach a few of the Indian children English so these ten children could then start teaching members of the tribe English. He wants his tribe to be able to speak the language in case the government tries to do something with them," Dan explained.

Jacob sighed as he heard the explanation. He thought it was a rather good idea and he could reasonably see the benefits for Brown Bear and his people if they all understood English. However, Jacob could already foresee the possible issues with the Indian children being in town each school day. He'd already witnessed such an instance and would have liked to have been forewarned about the situation beforehand in order to keep an eye out for such a thing.

"I get what you're trying to do here, Dan, but I just wish you would have told me sooner. Tanner and I can keep an eye on the town hall so that no one gets a wise idea about their own ill way of thinking," Jacob said.

"You're right, Sheriff. I should have told you because I know how passionate you are about keeping this town safe. I predicted that this type of thing would eventually happen. In all honesty, I was prepared to handle it myself," Dan explained. "I had told the Mayor about it before I even went to talk to Brown Bear."

"And I'm guessing the Mayor is supporting the idea?" Jacob asked.

"Yes. He still feels a sense of gratitude towards Brown Bear after what happened with the sickness not that long ago. And I feel the same way."

"As do I. If it wasn't for Brown Bear and White Raven, I'm confident I wouldn't have my Rosa with me today or the fact that soon we're going to be parents," Jacob said with a big grin. Dan couldn't help his own smile as the father-to-be beamed with joy at the thought of having a child soon.

"Well, Phoebe James has been helping me teach the Indian children English since she knows Sioux. She leads the children down the mountain from camp every morning and back every evening. It's been good to have the extra help during the day since I don't have my own way of communicating with the Indian children."

"That must be something, alright. I thought Miss James was too good to socialize with us simple townsfolk," Jacob said with a chuckle. He hadn't spent much time with Phoebe James but had talked plenty of times with her brother to ensure the peace between the miners and the Indian tribe.

"She's a mystery alright. My gut tells me there's something in her past keeping her from really opening up," Dan said. He wasn't about to argue with the Sheriff that Phoebe was more than what most people thought of her. He reasoned that in time the town's people would warm up to Phoebe, especially since she was spending more time in town.

"Well, as I always say, stick with your gut. You never know where it will lead you," Jacob said with a wink. He wondered if there was anything more between Phoebe and Dan than the man was leading on. But he figured he'd know if things became official. "You have a good rest of your day, Mr. Mavis. I'll be sure to be of a helping hand if things ever do get out of hand."

"I appreciate it, Sheriff. You have a good day as well," Dan said before Jacob turned and left the town hall. Dan watched him go, thinking that it was good to have the Sheriff on his side. With his right arm fully healed, Jacob was as good a shot as ever. It was important to stay in the good graces of such a man.

Returning to his notes, Dan sat down at his desk and tried to finish his work before anything he wanted to write down left his mind. His thoughts battled with one another because he was thinking about what had happened today with the parents mixed in with the fact that Phoebe had agreed to meet him for dinner tomorrow. He was certainly excited about the dinner date but unnerved that, already in the first week, he was having a confrontation with parents. And, it appeared that Mr. Miller was quick to wrangle together the help of other fathers. It seemed to Dan that Mr. Miller at the moment was his biggest threat to teaching the Indian children.

CHAPTER 6

*B*y the time Phoebe returned to camp with the Indian children, she'd already finished talking to them about what had happened today outside of the town hall. She'd first explained what the men had been doing and finally why.

"I don't know why those fathers were so angry. I like to play with the other children and practice speaking English with them," Grasshopper said to her in Sioux as they rode high into the mountains.

"White men think they can control anything they want to," Phoebe explained. "You are very lucky to have a kind school-teacher. There are not many men like Mr. Mavis."

The children chuckled at her comment and she had to really look at them to understand why they thought that was so funny. She had a sneaking suspicion and wasn't about to comment on that right now.

When they reached the camp, she gave them all a small hug before dismissing them back to their families. She always felt good at the end of the afternoon to see them happily go off and meet up with their parents and siblings. Phoebe knew that the children would speak to their parents about what happened today, and before anyone could question her, she went in search of Brown Bear.

Normally Phoebe was able to find Brown Bear near the central fire, but today she had to really go in search of him. She eventually found him standing near the corral, watching the Indian ponies race around the area as they nipped and played with one another.

"Good afternoon, Brown Bear," Phoebe said in Sioux as she approached him. "Why are you watching the ponies?"

"Hello, Phoebe," Brown Bear greeted her as he turned to her with a small smile on his face. "I like to watch the ponies from time to time because they are so carefree. They run and play with no thoughts to when their next meal will be. They know that someone will come to feed them and therefore they worry about very little."

"It sounds as though you've been worrying a lot and have now come to find a moment of not worrying at all," Phoebe mused.

"You're very smart," Brown Bear said with a chuckle. "I forget sometimes how intelligent White women can be in matters of conversation. Though I'd trust an Indian maiden as I would one of my braves, White women have become a creature of their own." This time it was Phoebe's time to chuckle at the perspective the Indian chief had of her.

"So, Brown Bear. What has you troubled?"

He sighed as he looked back at the ponies racing around the corral. Brown Bear knew it wasn't time to share his worries with Phoebe. The truth of it all would be known eventually. The Mayor of Bear Creek knew what he was facing and therefore Brown Bear figured that it was enough for now.

"I'm more curious about the children who have been studying English this week. How are their lessons?" Brown Bear asked. Phoebe could tell the Indian chief was ignoring her question and therefore she decided not to press her luck with him.

"The children are fast learners. Both Mr. Mavis and I are very impressed by how quickly they are learning. They are eager to learn and understand the grand responsibility they have been given. They take their lessons very seriously."

"Good. This I am pleased to hear."

"However, today at the end of their lessons, some of the children of Bear Creek were met by their fathers outside the town hall. These few fathers had come to voice their opinion that they were not pleased the Indian children were being taught English."

"What happened?" Brown Bear asked, very concerned.

"Mr. Mavis spoke to them and turned them away. You would have been very impressed with his ability to fight these men with only his words." The way Phoebe spoke of the schoolteacher made Brown Bear wonder if she was starting to develop strong feelings for the man. He smirked as well as he thought about getting to see Dan Mavis speak with such strong words since he didn't appear to be a physically strong man.

"I would have very much liked to have seen this. I am glad that Mr. Mavis was able to handle the situation. But do you fear that this will happen again?" Brown Bear asked.

"I cannot say, but I reasonably think that something will happen again because of the prejudice of the townspeople. And, the Indian children will tell their parents of what has happened. I have spoken to the children already and explained what had happened and why. I am certain that both you and I will have more angry parents on our hands from the children's mothers."

Brown Bear sighed as he nodded. He knew that Phoebe was both a wise woman and very logical. It seemed that he needed to prepare himself to talk to the parents of the children he had chosen for this arrangement.

"Then I shall go and face the raging waters before they completely wash away any goodness that will come from this arrangement," Brown Bear said with a grunt, signaling to Phoebe that he was done speaking and would go now. Phoebe didn't try to continue the conversation or say anymore as she turned from Brown Bear and returned to her horse. She wanted to return to her and her brother's cabin to freshen up before returning to town for the book club meeting. She was looking forward to it, and even looking forward to seeing Dan again even though they'd just spent the entire day together.

THE EVENING WAS in full swing as Dan waited patiently for his club members to arrive at the town hall. The sun had set and so Dan had lit several candles around the town hall to create plenty of light. Hanging on the hook outside the main door was a lantern so that the members knew that he was ready for the book club. But as six-thirty came and went, Dan began to wonder where everyone was that night.

Dan got up from his chair and walked through the town hall to the front. There, he stood in the doorway and looked out into the darkness that had settled over the town. A few other businesses hung a lantern out front of their shops, like the inn that was always open and welcome for visitors, and also the barbershop that stayed open late for the farmers and cattle ranchers that needed a haircut after working hours. And when Dr. Harvey was in the clinic late at night, he'd also leave a lantern outside the clinic.

The sound of hooves hitting the road came from in the

distance. Dan looked down the road leaving town to the south to see a wagon coming up the road. In the light of the lantern, he realized that Mr. Fritz was driving a wagon with two mares pulling it. On the driver's seat next to him was Margret Phillips. Dan couldn't help but smile and wave as the two came closer, till Mr. Fritz pulled the mares to a stop in front of the town hall.

"Good evening, Mr. Mavis," Margret said in a cheerful voice. "Do forgive us for being so late this evening." Mr. Fritz put the wheel peg into the wheel to prevent the wagon from rolling away before getting down from the driver's seat and going around the wagon to help Margret down. Dan saw how much of a gentleman Mr. Fritz could be and figured that what Mathew and Jenny had said was true. It seemed that the banker was smitten with the widow.

"You two are not late at all," Dan said as he found his voice once more. "It seems as though the others are also going to be late or unable to make it this evening."

"That's rather odd," Margret said as she walked up the stairs with her arm placed on Mr. Fritz's. "Usually the others always come."

The sound of more hooves hitting the ground could be heard and they all looked to the north as Phoebe James came riding into town. Dan's heartbeat increased as he saw her. He couldn't contain his own smile as she stopped her horse at the town hall and promptly dismounted.

"Just in time," Dan said to her in greeting. "It seems it shall just be the four of us this evening."

"Then I shall simply have more time to talk of my own opinion," Phoebe said cheerfully. Dan ushered in the group and closed the door behind them. Then, they sat in the pews or other chairs, discussing their current novel. In two weeks, they'd complete the book and then have to decide on another. And since

Mr. Fritz hadn't read the current novel at all, he was simply pleased to listen to the others speak. It was primarily Margret and Phoebe discussing their recently read chapters, giving the two men ample time to listen and observe the woman that interested them more than the book.

"What do you think, Mr. Mavis? Is Caroline being unreasonable with her demands to Mr. Harker? Or, is the author trying to convey a certain message about women in general?" Phoebe asked. Dan had been so consumed by his thoughts of Phoebe that at first he hadn't realized that the question was directed towards him.

"Well, umm, let's see here," Dan said as he started to flip through the book to the section in question. "Caroline is simply wanting to understand Mr. Harker and his demands. So, when she poses her own demands in return, she can appear quite unreasonable. I simply think that Caroline is a woman who knows what she wants and isn't willing to adjust those wants to fit the needs of someone else."

"I think it's Caroline's way of testing Mr. Harker," Margret then said. "As though she wants to see just how willing or unwilling he is to change his ways." Dan watched as Margret gave Mr. Fritz a stern look with her chin raised and, if he had been further away, he would have chuckled to himself. But this time he held his tongue as he looked away and instead started to focus on Phoebe once more. He found her watching him again and he thought he was starting to appreciate the attention from such a beautiful woman. Perhaps he wouldn't have to keep his mail-order-bride ad after all.

"There are several books we can choose from after this one," Dan said as he moved the conversation forward. "I'm wondering though if we should wait till next Friday when the majority of the members are present."

"Let's wait till next week. I'm sure that they were just busy and will be able to attend the following week," Phoebe suggested. "Though I am eager to hear about the possible books you'd be able to suggest for the book club."

"All in good time, Miss James," Dan said with a smile. "Well, I think that's it for this evening. I look forward to hearing your opinions once more about our current novel next Friday." Dan then stood and put away his chair before leading the members out the front door. It was good to see Margret and Mr. Fritz share a loving look as they walked down the aisle together, arm in arm. He could easily see them tying the knot one day.

"See you tomorrow, Dan," Phoebe said in a soft voice before she walked out of the doors of the town hall. Dan was the last to leave and he made sure to pull the doors closed behind him and lock up before making his own way home. He was certainly looking forward to seeing Phoebe tomorrow for their date.

"Good night," Dan called out to everyone, waiting a moment to see that they headed out of town alright. He didn't like the idea of Phoebe riding alone at night. He hoped that she wouldn't run into any trouble along her way. No matter how familiar she was with the trail, he'd still worry about any woman riding alone at night.

Dan was so eager for tomorrow that he made quick work of gathering his mare from the livery stables and making his way home. Though the way was dark, the openness of the plains allowed him to see far into the distance with only the moonlight to guide his way. There was something mystical about being alone on a warm night, nothing but the stillness of the night to greet him.

By the time he returned to his cottage, Dan was eager to retire for the night. The day had been long, and though he was pleased to have arranged a dinner date with Phoebe, the thoughts of Mr. Miller returned to his mind as he put his mare in her stall and got her ready for the night. Then, Dan made his way inside his cottage and fixed himself something small to eat before heading to bed. All the while, he thought of Mr. Miller and wondered if the man would pose any more threats to him or the Indian children. He didn't agree with the man one bit and hoped that the father wouldn't try to persuade anyone else to his line of thinking, either.

As Dan lay in bed, he tried to focus on the positive of seeing Phoebe tomorrow and getting to share a meal with her. He was truly interested in learning some Sioux words and thought it would be interesting to surprise the Indian children come Monday with the things he had learned. It would be his way of showing all the children that he was truly dedicated in teaching them all and that even he was able to learn new things from time to time.

But really occupying Dan's thoughts was Mr. Miller. He hoped beyond belief that he wouldn't have to deal with the man again. He didn't want any trouble, and he certainly didn't want that type of environment for any of his children. As Dan said his prayers that night, he prayed for Gravis and the Miller family, that their hearts might be softened. Then, he prayed that he'd have a good meal with Phoebe and that perhaps he'd one day be able to tell her his true feelings.

CHAPTER 7

*A*fter spending the entire week rising extra early, Phoebe took her time Saturday morning waking up. She'd slept in well past the rising of the sun and leisurely stretched before getting out of bed. It would have been the type of thing she'd be used to on a daily basis if she still lived in Boston with her parents. Now, with so much to do every day just to keep food on the table and living in a clean house, Phoebe rarely allowed herself the opportunity to sleep in. But after working so hard all week with the Indian children, she figured she'd earned a little extra rest on a Saturday morning.

Once she'd gotten out of bed and readied herself for the day, Phoebe made her way into the main room of the cabin. She sighed, wishing they could live in a more suitable house closer to town. But with Edward coming home each evening covered in soot, she figured that she wouldn't want him traveling through the forest at night just to get home or covering their nice house in all his filth.

Phoebe made her way into the kitchen part of the cabin to see that Edward had already gone for the day. He'd left her some coffee in the kettle, and she poured herself the rest of the liquid in a tin cup and sipped it slowly. She didn't like the bitter taste of coffee, but she also didn't have the opportunity to make herself a proper cup of tea in the morning. And if she wanted milk, she'd have to go into town or go and visit one of the ranch farms to get any. There were many drawbacks of living in the mountains and, on most days, she tried very hard not to focus on all of them.

The morning came and went as Phoebe made herself a modest breakfast of toast and eggs before doing her best to clean the cabin properly. She washed the dishes, dried them and put them in the cupboards. Then, she swept the cabin and did her best to even mop the floors. It took several buckets of water, but by the time the afternoon came, she was pleased with all that she was able to accomplish. She even quickly washed some of their laundry and hung it out to dry before she started to think about her attire for the evening.

Phoebe knew that her date with Dan was only to allow him the opportunity to learn some Sioux words. Though she still stood by her idea that Dan would learn more if he spent more time at the Indian camp, she thought it would be nice to dine out for once. Back in Boston, she was used to dining out at least three times a week. It was either dinner parties or restaurant dates that she would attend with her parents. Moving to Bear Creek had not only forced her to eat dishes she'd never considered before, but she also had to learn to cook with the ingredients she could gather up from either town or a few of their friends.

Even though there was much she missed about Boston and the way her life used to be, she had no regrets about moving to Bear Creek. Every time the images of her past surfaced, it reminded her why they'd needed to leave Boston as soon as possible without any sort of intention to return. Edward had finally been ousted from society once it became clear that their father had slept with an Indian woman during one of his travels West for 'business'. Though Mrs. James had raised Edward as her own, it became clear in his late youth as he started to become more of a man that he didn't really look like either of his parents. It had been a very dark and rainy night when Mr. James had confessed all to his son, causing him to flee Boston and seek out his real mother.

It was only when Phoebe found herself in some deep trouble that Edward returned. He had only done it to save her, and when he promised her a better life, she took it without looking back. Boston might have provided her an easier way of living, but it hadn't been able to show her how to truly live.

"No point rekindling the past," Phoebe said to herself as she started to look through her wardrobe for something suitable to wear. She didn't want to wear her best dress in case she gave the wrong impression to Dan. After all, this was just a learning opportunity for him. But she also didn't want to wear something she normally did. It would be nice to dress up for once because she rarely got the opportunity to do it anymore. She even took the time to curl her hair with rollers and pins before teasing it up into an up-do.

"Suitable enough, I suppose," Phoebe said to her reflection as she turned her head from side to side in the looking glass hanging on the wall behind her dresser. The mirror was rather small, but it helped her finish the look she had been working towards. Phoebe didn't let her mind wander to the type of gowns she used to wear on a daily basis, often changing into two or three gowns a day depending on what had been planned. Phoebe turned her back on the looking glass and all the past memories it reflected as she made her way out of her room and towards the front door.

Before she could reach it, Edward opened it and came walking in, covered in the dirt of the mountain tunnels. If she didn't know her brother well, she would have mistaken him for an intruder. His dark obsidian hair was tied back, his dark skin covered in dirt and soot.

"Well, well. Where are you off to, Sis?" Edward said with a smile as he shut the door behind him and started pulling off his boots. His goal was to track the least amount of dirt and soot into the house as possible. But he'd need to cross the main room to reach his bedroom to start washing off all the grime. But seeing his sister dressed up in the evening made him wonder what she was up to.

"I have an appointment with Dan Mavis. He wishes to learn some Sioux words to better understand the Indian children," Phoebe explained as she folded her hands before her and straightened her posture. She looked at Edward without letting her eyes drift away so that he could not make any assumptions about her plans.

"Sounds like the schoolteacher is really willing to help out the Sioux kids," Edward said as he finished pulling off his boots before unbuttoning his outer work shirt.

"After working with Dan this week, I can tell that his intentions are genuine. I think that it's wise for him to learn a bit of Sioux as the Indian children begin learning English. It will show the children that he's as dedicated as they are."

"Well, don't let me stop you from your appointment," Edward said as he stepped around Phoebe, afraid that the dirt he was covered in would somehow get on her nice gown. "Is he meeting you at the camp?"

"At the inn," Phoebe replied as she turned towards him, fearing this would be the part in their conversation where he would start to speculate. "We are having dinner together."

Edward stopped his progress towards his room and turned to face his sister. "Like a date?" he asked.

"I suppose you could say that," Phoebe reasoned as she let her eyes drift from his, feeling suddenly nervous. "I suggested that in the future he comes to the Indian camp so he can truly learn easier."

"Wise advice," Edward said, his voice growing stern. "Do I need to talk to Dan about his intentions towards you?"

"What? No," Phoebe said as she met his gaze once more. "We're just having dinner, that's all. Dan has made no forward remarks to me that will let me know his feelings towards me if he has any. I just like the idea of dining out for once."

"If he becomes an issue, you just let me know," Edward said as he put his hands on his hips. "I'll be damned if I let another man treat you wrong."

Phoebe nodded, not wanting to discuss such things. She knew that Edward had every right to be protective of her. He'd come to her rescue once before and witnessed her in such a desperate state of despair that Phoebe was sure that the image had been burned into his memory. Phoebe knew she'd never forget it but hated to know that anyone else would forever share in her agony of what had happened to her.

"Enjoy your date, Phoebe," Edward said to break the silence that had settled between them. "I look forward to hearing all about it later tonight."

"Sure thing, Edward," Phoebe said as she looked at him briefly before heading out of the cabin. As she closed the front door behind her, she took a deep breath and let it out slowly. She wanted to have settled nerves before she reached town. After saddling her mare, Phoebe pulled herself onto the side-saddle and followed the trail that would lead her the quickest to town.

DAN COULDN'T DENY that he was a little nervous as he made his way into town. He'd left a bit early, wanting to arrive at the inn with plenty of time to choose the perfect table for his date with Phoebe. A part of him kept remembering that he was only meeting with her to learn Sioux. The other part was thrilled to be spending time practically alone with Phoebe. He was certain that he was the only man in town that had ever succeeded in convincing Phoebe to go on a date with him. Dan was surely feeling proud as he galloped into town.

After settling his horse at the livery stables, Dan crossed town and headed for the inn. The day was pretty warm with a light breeze sweeping through town. Dan knew that not too many more days would be filled with such warmth. Eventually the heat would break and give way to the fall when cold nights were quick to appear. And after the heavy snowfall they had last year, everyone in the area would sure to be stocking up for the winter months when too much snow fell to travel safely.

Teaching in the winters was the hardest thing for Dan. He already had such few students that when there was too much snow on the ground for all of them to travel into town, Dan knew that it was better to just cancel lessons until the roads were clear. With the Indian children attending lessons, he wondered how that would affect attendance for this winter since they had the furthest to travel.

Dan smiled at those he passed by on the boardwalk. He took his time, peering into different businesses and shops. He thought the town had really come alive ever since Edward James had purchased the mines and made them successful. He'd one day love to ask Edward what his secret was and how he was able to find all the precious gold that many had not been able to find before him. Dan knew that the mines had been opened for almost two generations, and the fact that they were still producing gold nuggets was indeed a surprise.

Eventually, Dan made it through town to the inn. He pulled open the door to the whitewashed building and found the space instantly inviting and warm. Ever since Rosa had come to Bear Creek as the Sheriff's mail-order-bride, she'd been helping out Mrs. Tibet in the kitchen since the Tibets were getting older in age. But Rosa had also made little changes around the inn, to include fresh wildflowers in various vases and new landscape paintings for the walls. It really livened up the place and made it more inviting than normal.

"Good afternoon, Mr. Mavis. How can I help you?" came Mr. Tibet's voice. Dan looked towards him and spotted him behind the check-in counter. The inn only had four rooms that were mostly rented to miners, but he was always willing to help a person if they truly needed a place to stay.

"Good afternoon, Mr. Tibet. I wanted to dine in this evening and was hoping to be able to pick out a table for my date," Dan explained in a hushed voice. He looked around the dining room that was rather large and across from the check-in counter. The inn often hosted many of the town's events, and newly married couples often had their reception at the inn.

"Ah, a special occasion I see," Mr. Tibet said with a bright smile. "You go on in and pick out which ever table you'd like. Who's the lucky lady so I know where to sit her when she comes in?"

"That would be Miss Phoebe James," Dan explained with a smirk on his lips. He almost laughed when Mr. Tibet raised his eyebrows in surprise.

"So, it seems the book-smart schoolteacher has tamed the

wild city girl," Mr. Tibet said in a hushed voice. Dan couldn't contain his laughter then and they both chuckled together.

"I'm not so sure about that, Mr. Tibet. But I do look forward to my evening with her," Dan admitted. He was about to explain the true nature of his date with Phoebe, but after remembering how Mr. Miller reacted yesterday, he figured that he'd better not start talking to everyone that he was teaching the Indian children in case it might ruin his date with Phoebe.

"Well, go on in and choose a table. I'll escort her in as soon as she arrives."

"Thank you, Mr. Tibet." Dan nodded to the older man and then turned and made his way into the dining room. After surveilling the few available tables, he picked one by a window. He figured he'd be able to see the sun setting from this position and it might add a bit of ambiance to their dinner.

Dan sat down at the table and did his best to take a deep breath to settle his nerves. The air came in and out of his lungs at a shaky pace and Dan knew he needed to get himself settled before Phoebe appeared. He tried to remind himself that there was no reason to be nervous or anxious. They'd spent all week together and were now meeting simply so he could start learning some common words in Sioux. But there was still that hope deep down inside that something more could come of this dinner date. He very much would like to continue these types of dates with Phoebe so he could perhaps someday gain enough courage to truly tell her how he felt about her.

Dan wasn't sure how much time had passed, but eventually Phoebe did appear. As he caught sight of Mr. Tibet escorting her over to the table, his heart began to thud hard against his chest. Dan did his best to contain his smile as he rose from the table as they came near.

"Good evening, Mr. Mavis," Phoebe said with a kind smile.

"Good evening," he replied as his eyes traveled over her. She was wearing a very fitting gown that showed off all the wonderful aspects of her body. But as their eyes met once more, Dan thought that her beautiful brown eyes were the best aspect of her because they held so much warmth and mystery.

Almost forgetting his manners, Dan pulled out Phoebe's chair and gestured for her to take a seat. Phoebe smiled softly as she allowed Dan to seat her. It was one of the things Phoebe liked most about Dan, is that he was a true gentleman. He wasn't just polite but considerate of others as well.

"I'll be right back with menus and water," Mr. Tibet said as he nodded towards Dan as the man sat back down in his chair. Mr. Tibet thought it was nice to a see a young couple getting together for dinner. He knew that Phoebe hadn't been to the inn to dine with any other man besides her brother when they first arrived at Bear Creek. He certainly was excited to tell Mrs. Tibet and Mrs. Benning the good news.

"How has your day been?" Dan asked once he was settled back down at the table. He was always awestruck at Phoebe's beauty and was pleased to think that he had a good excuse to look at her throughout the dinner.

"Oh, same old same old. Spent the day catching up on all the house chores since I've been spending most of my time either at the camp or here in town," Phoebe said. She realized that her life didn't sound hardly as exciting as it used to be.

"Nothing wrong with needing to catch up on things. I spent the day deep in notes and lesson ideas for the upcoming week. Really, it's nothing too exciting either," Dan said with a shrug of his shoulders. "Sometimes in life we simply have to spend a free day doing the things we must."

"Here you are," Mr. Tibet said as he returned with their menus and cups of water. "Mrs. Tibet has prepared a fine roast today and Mrs. Benning made something called a souffle. I haven't tried it yet, but she insists that it will taste good."

"My word, I would have not expected such a fine dish here in Bear Creek," Phoebe declared with a chuckle.

"Well, Mrs. Benning has certainly convinced Mrs. Tibet to try new things that she was used to in Boston," Mr. Tibet explained.

"I hadn't realized that Mrs. Benning was from Boston," Phoebe said in a soft voice. The very thought terrified her because she instantly wondered if Mrs. Benning therefore knew about her past already.

"Yuppery. She used to be a lady's maid for some big to-do family. Her charge even came and watched Rosa get married to the Sheriff before returning home with her father," Mr. Tibet explained. Suddenly, Phoebe felt panicked and wondered if she should return home. She certainly didn't want to run into a servant from Boston. Phoebe knew that all servants gossiped and knew the latest scandalous news before most people did.

"Would you like me to introduce you two?" Dan asked, watching Phoebe very closely. He'd seen the way she'd become excited over the idea of getting to eat souffle for dinner. But the mention of Boston had made her become very still and almost frightful.

"Oh no, that won't be necessary. But I'd certainly like to try her souffle," Phoebe said as she forced a smile back on her face. She wasn't about to let her nerves and past fears ruin the dinner date she was supposed to be having with Dan.

"And I'll try the roast," Dan said to Mr. Tibet as he handed back their menus. Once the older gentleman had left their table to go check on others, Dan turned his attention back to Phoebe with more curiosity about her than ever.

"So, are you ready for a short lesson while we wait on our

food?" Phoebe asked before Dan could steer their conversation away from the real reason they were here together.

"I'd love that," Dan said, knowing he'd have to wait for a more appropriate moment to ask Phoebe about her past.

For the next thirty minutes, Phoebe taught Dan a dozen words in Sioux. Though they were simple in meaning, from different greetings to asking one how they were that day, Dan's biggest problem was learning how to pronounce each word correctly. At one point, he became so tongue-tied that he made Phoebe snort with laughter.

"My goodness, forgive me," Phoebe said as her mirth started to subside. "That is perhaps the worst Sioux I have ever heard."

"Is it really that bad?" Dan asked with a chuckle.

"Oh yes, quite terrible. But I'm certain that with a little bit of practice that you'll be able to get it well enough to communicate with the children," Phoebe said in hopes of encouraging him not to give up. She had taken a long time to learn the language, but after two years, she'd been able to learn pretty quickly since she spent so much time at the Indian camp.

It was then that their dinner arrived. Phoebe was delighted to see the souffle in its own container, perfectly raised from the oven without the top deflating at all. She was eager to try it and see if it tasted like anything she remembered. She picked up her fork and knife and cut carefully into the top flaky layers to reveal the warm center. She wasn't sure what savory meat it was filled with, but as Phoebe prepared her first bite with enough inner mixture paired with the outer flaky crust, she only grew more excited to try it.

Placing the fork in her mouth, she let the delightful flavors wash over her. It brought back so many good memories as she closed her eyes for a moment and relished in the taste of it all. Phoebe had been certain that she wouldn't have the opportunity to taste any of the fine dishes from her past, but yet here she was sitting in a country inn eating a wonderfully cooked souffle.

Dan ate a bite of his roast beef and watched Phoebe enjoy her food, wondering if he should have ordered the souffle as well. Dan hadn't seen Phoebe make such a face as she seemed to thoroughly enjoy each and every bite of the souffle, even closing her eyes and sighing with pleasure from time to time. He liked to see such expression on her face as though she was experiencing pure bliss.

"I can't help but tell just how much you're enjoying that," Dan said with a smile. Phoebe looked at him, almost forgetting that she was surrounded by other people as she became lost in her own thoughts and feelings.

She patted her lips on the cloth napkin before saying, "Forgive me. I had not expected it to taste that good."

"No need to apologize. Just makes me regret ordering the roast."

"I will agree that it should be a rather large regret. This has been cooked perfectly. It's such a complicated dish because the top can deflate if it's not cooked in a proper temperature and left to cook slowly. It's rich and warm with a very flaky crust. This is really something I would expect from a restaurant in Boston."

"I'm guessing there are some things about Boston that you truly miss," Dan said, thinking he'd found his opportunity to ask more pertinent questions about her past.

Phoebe shrugged her shoulders as she savored another bite. When she'd finished that bite, she said, "Boston is simply different than Bear Creek. One is a city while the other is a small town. Boston simply has more of everything and a wide variety."

"That is very true. But I'm sure your lifestyle was different as well. From what I've gathered, you're classically educated, and must come from a well-off family. Certainly you weren't previously a lady's maid like Mrs. Benning was." Phoebe took a long drink of her water, trying to gather her thoughts. Dan wasn't like the other men she knew from Bear Creek. He was intellectual and could probably see through any disguise she tried to put up to avoid talking about her past.

"No, I was never a lady's maid. But I did have a few of them," Phoebe said with a soft smile. "My life in Boston was drastically different from what I experience today. Yes, there are some things I miss about Boston and that life, but there is in no way that I regret coming to Bear Creek." Dan stilled for a moment, trying to think just how wealthy Phoebe's parents must be if she had several maids at her disposal. It made Dan curious to know what had happened in her past to force her to leave everything she knew behind and make living in the country a very reasonable exchange.

"You must certainly have learned a lot by coming to live in Bear Creek. And the mountains, no doubt," Dan said with a smile. He wanted to keep the conversation positive and not focus too much on the reason she left Boston.

"Oh yes, indeed," Phoebe said with a chuckle. "All manner of cooking and cleaning, fetching my own water, raising my own chickens. These are things I certainly was never educated on, but thankfully Edward made for a good teacher."

"I'm glad to hear that. I've spent very little time with either you or your brother that I haven't created a solid opinion of Mr. James," Dan admitted.

"Please, just call him Edward. Mr. James was our father and neither one of us like to be reminded of the man," Phoebe said in a soft voice.

"Duly noted," Dan said as he nodded. "I shall avoid making such a mistake in the future."

Phoebe could hardly believe how kind and considerate Dan

was being. Unlike most people she talked about her past with, Dan wasn't pressing or needing to know what had happened. He'd even steered the conversation away from her past and tried to focus on more recent events. Their conversation continued as she described more about what she'd come to learn about since coming to Bear Creek and how much she enjoyed visiting the Indian camp to be around those people.

"What I love most about the Sioux is that they all work together. It doesn't matter who your parents are and anyone's past mistakes. They all make sure that everyone in the tribe has enough. The men all hunt together, the women all cook together. Everyone in the tribe eats the same thing together and works hard to take care of one another. It's a sense of community that I thoroughly enjoy. I can just go to camp and just jump right in with what the other women are currently doing."

"What things do you often do with the Indian women?" Dan asked, liking how excited she began to talk when she described things she really enjoyed. It was the type of happiness that he hoped to instill in Phoebe any chance he was able to.

"Well, I've come to enjoy bead work. The beads are made out of clay and hand painted. I like to use them to either make jewelry or help one of the women use the beads in different ceremonial clothes. There is something about creating things with my hands that really brings me joy."

"I feel the same way when it comes to teaching. Every time one of my students learns a new skill or gets a math question correct that they've gotten wrong in the past really brings me joy. I love to help people and I love to help them learn the most."

Dan and Phoebe smiled at one another as they came to realize something that they both had in common. A sense of accomplishment and the pride from succeeding was something they both understood. Phoebe simply wondered if she could ever tell Dan the reason why it meant so much to her. In Boston, during her previous lifestyle, everything she ever wanted or needed was given to her by simply asking one of her maids. She'd never had to work for anything before and certainly never created anything of her own. Now, she could make all sorts of things and give them to people that she really cared about.

As the meal came to an end, Dan paid for their food before escorting Phoebe outside. They bid Mr. Tibet farewell before stepping outside. The warm evening breeze felt good on Phoebe's skin and she looked forward to her journey back to the cabin. She was excited to tell her brother how well the evening had gone and perhaps how her own feelings were changing towards Dan Mavis.

"I hope you enjoyed yourself," Dan said as he walked with Phoebe to the livery stables so they could both collect their horses.

"I'm sure my face told all," Phoebe said with a chuckle. "That souffle was to die for. I do hope Mrs. Benning will cook it more often. It makes me think that I should dine in town more frequently just to see what she's cooking up." Dan couldn't help but chuckle, glad to hear that Phoebe had enjoyed the dinner.

"If you ever need someone to dine with, I'd be happy to accompany you," Dan offered, hoping he wasn't being too forward. However, he at least wanted Phoebe to get the idea that he was interested in spending more time with her.

"I think we could make that arrangement," Phoebe said with a smile. "And perhaps you would like to come to the camp to have dinner with all of us there."

"Just let me know when and I'll be there."

"Around five o'clock tomorrow," Phoebe quickly replied, wondering how far she could test Dan's words.

"Then five o'clock tomorrow it is," Dan agreed. "Mrs. Jenkins once told me that the blood soup is actually delicious."

"Despite the name, it actually is." Phoebe and Dan laughed together as they entered the stables. Dan helped Phoebe ready her mare, but before she pulled herself up into the saddle, Dan touched her shoulder to stop her. Phoebe turned and looked up into Dan's eyes, wondering what he wanted to say to her as her heart beat started to increase.

"Phoebe, may I kiss you?" Dan asked in a soft voice, his blue eyes searching hers to see if he'd said the wrong thing or at least asked the question too soon.

"Perhaps on the cheek wouldn't be too terrible of an idea," Phoebe replied with wide eyes. She hadn't expected Dan to ask her such a question, but now that she thought about it, she wondered what it would be like to feel Dan kiss her. She stilled as he leaned down and slowly placed a kiss on her cheek. She felt the warmth of his lips on her skin and instantly wondered what it would feel like to press her lips up against his.

As Dan lifted his lips from her cheek, Phoebe wished that he would have remained close to her. But he created the appropriate distance between them as he let his hand drop from her shoulder. He gave her a kind smile as he then helped her up onto her side-saddle. She was perfectly speechless as she smiled down at Dan and gave him a little wave before clicking her tongue. Phoebe coaxed her mare out of the stables, but as they reached the barn door, she turned and waved at Dan once more.

Dan could hardly believe he'd been so bold as to ask Phoebe to let him kiss her. He stood there in the stables, a lopsided grin on his face as he waved back at Phoebe. He'd just placed a kiss on the cheek of the woman he was quickly falling for. He was very certain no man in town had been so privileged, and the fact that he'd be seeing her once again tomorrow only made the moment that much grander. As Dan saddled his own horse with the preparations to head home to his cottage, he surely could not wait for tomorrow and to experience a traditional Indian meal with Phoebe. Maybe he could steal another kiss from her as soon as tomorrow, the idea causing him to smile all the way home.

CHAPTER 8

With each passing day, Dan's affections for Phoebe only continued to grow. He enjoyed the private moments that they got to spend together either at the Indian camp or in town as they did more things together. Phoebe enjoyed showing Dan through the forest in the mountains and through the Indian camp. He was certainly learning more Sioux words each day, which only made his students even more surprised. He enjoyed teasing the Indian children in Sioux and even teaching the other children a few of the words so they could talk to their new friends easier.

When he was alone with Phoebe, he would always ask her permission before he either kissed her or simply held her hand. There was something about asking her permission first that always seemed to cause Phoebe to relax and accept his gesture of affection. From time to time, especially when they parted, she would even place a kiss of her own on the back of his knuckles or on his cheek. It was moments like this that Dan was certainly glad that he'd gathered up the courage to ask Phoebe on a date and even kiss her before seeing her return home.

His days in the town hall teaching were filled with even more joy than normal because he got to spend them also with Phoebe. Together, they really helped each of the students learn their lessons. He found it was easier to teach when he had an assistant, and the children really liked having another person to ask for help or to learn from. Even the Indian children were seeming to really like the lessons and would practice their English with the other students every chance they got.

Thankfully, there had been no more trouble from Mr. Miller. Dan also didn't hear any comments from the town's people. And for the longest of weeks, as summer finally came to an end and fall began, life seemed to be pretty peaceful. At least, until that fateful Friday in September when everything seemed to change suddenly for Dan.

Dan was right in the middle of explaining what a compound sentence was to the students when the doors of the town hall were thrown open. The loud banging of the doors against the wall made Dan halt in his lecture as all eyes turned to the person that had just stumbled into the building. Fiery red hair graced the top of this woman's head as she came hurrying into the town hall with a large trunk in her hands. Her green eyes were wide with excitement as she fixed them on Dan. Just her wild appearance made Dan apprehensive about this woman who seemed thrilled to see him.

"Are you Dan Mavis?" she asked as she set her trunk down with a thud in front of him, making him jump.

"Umm, yes?" Dan replied as he looked her up and down. She was a petite woman with a worn traveling gown and boots. He'd never seen her before and wondered why on earth she knew his name.

"Oh, thank the Good Lord. I've been riding for weeks to finally come and meet you. Got caught up along the way from Indiana but I'm finally here to be your mail-order-bride!" she said enthusiastically, and more dreadfully, very loudly. Dan's eyes grew wide at her words as he tried hard to remember if he'd ever received a letter from this woman. And when she stood on her trunk and wrapped her arms around him, he became very alarmed as the students all began to laugh.

"Miss, I have no idea who you are," Dan said as he pulled her arms off of him and stood back from her. She stepped off her trunk and continued to pursue him, obviously unaware that there were many eyes on them. Even the Mayor had stepped out of his office to see what all the noise was about.

"Forgive me, where are my manners? My name's Nancy Tender from Indiana. I saw your mail-order-bride ad in the news-paper on the most frightening day of my life. I just knew that I needed to come straight to Bear Creek to be your wife. I'm sorry I never took the time to write. My handwriting isn't the best. My goodness, I am so excited to finally meet you. I've been dreaming of this moment ever since I left my horrible home and began thinking of such a bright future with you."

Dan seriously thought he was dreaming. How could this have happened and why would Nancy gain the impression from his ad that he was this desperate for a wife, any wife? He looked past Nancy and met Phoebe's eyes. He could see tears in them as her face had gone a deathly pale. She was speaking softly to the Indian children. And as he saw them begin to stand, he figured she'd told them it was time to go home.

Dan walked around Nancy, avoiding her hand as she reached out to him. He focused on the students as he said, "Please be excused for the rest of the day. It appears I have a matter I must deal with that can't be postponed till later. Since it is Friday and

we won't be meeting again till Monday, please continue practicing your sentences. Take the time to do a bit of reading as
well."

Dan said goodbye to all the students as they slowly rose and
left the town hall. They were obviously curious about what was
going on and also excited about getting to leave a bit early. Dan
said goodbye to the Indian children in their native language, but
when he went to speak with Phoebe, she didn't give him the
opportunity. She quickly followed the children out of the town
hall, pulling the door closed behind her.

Dan sighed as he met the Mayor's eyes. The man raised his
eyebrows at Dan and all he could think to do was shrug his
shoulders. Mr. Franklin pointed to his office before heading that
way, indicating to Dan that he was only just around the corner if
he needed anything. Dan simply nodded to the man before
turning around and returning to the redheaded woman.

"Alright, Miss Tender. You now have my full attention," Dan
said as he approached her. She was still standing there with
wide, excited eyes that seemed to search his face for
reassurance.

"Mr. Mavis, I just know I'll make the perfect wife for you. I
can cook and clean, and people say I'm loads of fun and always
great to laugh with," Nancy said with a proud smile.

"Miss Tender, I'm not about to marry a woman I have never
met before. Though I don't discredit your values, you must
understand how very sudden this all is," Dan said, trying to be
careful with what words he spoke to the lady. It was a long
distance from Bear Creek to Indiana. He couldn't imagine
making that journey alone and wasn't even sure how Nancy had
made her way to Bear Creek.

"Oh, don't worry, Mr. Mavis. I have no other place to go and
therefore we shall have all the time in the world to get to know

one another. I'm certain you'll be falling in love with me before too long," she said with a giggle.

"Miss Tender, why did you leave your home so suddenly? You said you saw my ad on a most terrible night," Dan said.

"Oh, Mr. Mavis. You'll surely not believe me. But my father was a drunk and a very abusive man. He'd beat me a lot when he was in the mood. And right before I left it all behind me, he seemed to be in the mood quite a bit to hit me." Nancy seemed to settle down as she spoke about her abusive father. She became very quiet as she looked at Dan with pleading eyes.

"I'm so sorry to hear that, Miss Tender. I don't blame you for leaving Indiana behind and going somewhere you could feel safe. Have you eaten? Do you need a place to rest from your travels?"

"Oh yes, I'm famished. I've been on the road for so long that I can't wait to get settled down at your place," Nancy said as her bright smile returned.

"Well, it wouldn't be proper for two unmarried people to be living together. How about I take your trunk and I'll show you to the local inn. Mr. and Mrs. Tibet are a wonderful couple and they keep a fine establishment. Mrs. Tibet is a wonderful cook and could make you a plate of food rather quickly."

"Alright. I suppose that will be fine till we're married." Dan was becoming rather frustrated with this woman as he bent down and picked up her trunk. Thankfully it was light and he was able to carry it with ease as he led Nancy from the town hall and across town to the inn. He wanted to get Nancy settled as soon as possible so he could go tell Phoebe what had truly happened. He didn't want to give her the wrong idea about him, but he would have to deal with one problem at a time.

"My, my, Bear Creek is such a pleasant little place. I could see myself getting married here and raising a little family of my own," Nancy said as she looked around and took in the quaint town. She saw that it didn't have much, but compared to the place she'd just left, she'd take anything if it meant she could be happy and safe. Just traveling these last few weeks had been life changing for Nancy as she met all sorts of people and stayed at wonderful inns along the way. But if she was being honest, her savings were starting to run low.

"It's a wonderful town. I'm sure you could settle down here," Dan said, trying to remain positive.

"Absolutely. Once we're married, I think I'll finally feel content after a long life of physical abuse," Nancy said as she focused her eyes back on Dan. "I used to work at a general store and saved up all my money so one day I could leave. Once I saw your ad, it gave me the motivation to finally do it. Had to steal my father's horse, but I finally made it to meet you." She looped her arm around his and had he not been carrying her trunk he would have pulled away from her.

And so, as Dan entered the inn, he did so with a strange woman on his arm and her things in his hands. Mr. Tibet looked up from the counter and gave him a puzzled look as he came forward. Dan finally set the trunk down in front of the counter and pulled Nancy's hand from his arm as he gave her a disapproving look. She simply giggled before looking at the man behind the counter.

"Mr. Tibet, this is Nancy Tender. She's just arrived in town and will be needing a room," Dan said in a depressing tone. He hated to explain the situation to anyone else because he was already very embarrassed.

"There's the women's room just down the hallway, the same one that Rosa used when she first came to town. Might I inquire if you'll be staying long at the inn?" Mr. Tibet asked as he looked at Nancy.

"Not long. Mr. Mavis and I shall be married shortly so I'm sure I'll be moving in with him before too long," Nancy happily said. Dan groaned as he turned and looked down at Nancy.

"Miss Tender, I have not made you an offer of marriage. Though I'm glad you are safe and away from your previous situation, it would not be proper to tell people we are intended when we are not," Dan said as he did his best not to lose his temper.

"Don't worry, Mr. Mavis. I won't give you any reason not to quickly propose," she said with a chuckle.

"Alright then, Miss Tender. Let's get you settled in," Mr. Tibet said as he quickly gave Nancy the key and showed her to her room. From where Dan stood at the counter, he could hear her squeal with delight as she entered the room. It only made Dan groan more as he thought that Nancy would be the last person he'd ever consider for a wife.

Mr. Tibet quickly returned for Nancy's trunk but paused to ask Dan, "Mr. Mavis, what on earth is going on?"

"Mr. Tibet, I do wish I understood. It seems that Miss Tender saw my mail-order-bride ad in the papers in Indiana and thought I would be desperate enough for a wife that I would just accept her on the spot."

"Son, I think you're in a world of trouble, especially since I already know you and Miss James have been frequently seeing each other."

"Believe me. I know. Miss Tender came barging into the town hall and practically threw herself at me while I was in the middle of teaching the children. Phoebe saw it all and she didn't look so happy to see Miss Tender."

"Well, I don't blame Miss James one bit. But what are you going to do with Nancy?" Mr. Tibet asked as he picked up her trunk.

"I'm not sure at the moment, but could you keep her busy for a bit? Have Mrs. Tibet make her a plate of food and I'll cover the bill if she can't," Dan said. "I'll be back later this afternoon with a plan. After all, if she wants to get married real quick, there is plenty of eligible men in this town."

"And that's no joke," Mr. Tibet said. "Well, I'll see what I can do."

"Thank you, Mr. Tibet." Dan watched as the older man carried the trunk to the room, speaking to Nancy long enough that Dan was able to slip out the front door and disappear before he could be stopped by the strange woman again.

"What a mess," Dan mumbled to himself as he made his way back to the town hall. As soon as he stepped in through the door, however, the Mayor was quick to stop him.

"Hey, Dan. Everything okay?" he asked as he quickly went around the desk to greet him. The Mayor had left his office door open so he could stop Dan the moment the man returned. He'd never seen anything like the scene he'd just witnessed and wanted to make sure his friend was doing alright.

"Yes, Mr. Franklin. Everything is okay. I just think there's been a huge mistake is all," Dan said as he stopped to talk to the Mayor.

"That woman looked awfully happy to see you," the Mayor observed. He rubbed his chin as he gave Dan a very critical look. "Have you been messing around behind Phoebe's back?"

"For goodness sake, no, Mr. Franklin," Dan said very sternly. His temper was flaring back up again and he wasn't sure how much more he could take. "I've never seen that woman before in my life. She says she saw my mail-order-bride ad and came all this way to marry me. But she never wrote to me or received my consent to do so."

"Mail-order-bride ad? I didn't know you had placed one."

"Well, I didn't think I had any other option. Never thought in a million years that Phoebe would agree to go out on a date with me, let alone let me kiss her," Dan rambled. He didn't mean to have said that last part and grimaced as the Mayor smiled brightly at him. "Anyways, I had placed the ad a while back but hadn't received any letters in a while. Plus, things had been going well between Phoebe and me."

"Have you had a chance to talk to Phoebe yet about the whole mix up?"

"Not yet. Figure I have to put out one fire before I can put out the other. I'm going to go straight over to Fry's now to send a telegram to have my ad removed from the *Matrimonial Times*. Then I need to figure out what to tell Nancy."

"If she's looking to get married, she's come to the right spot. Bear Creek has plenty of single men and not enough single women."

"Mr. Tibet mentioned the same thing. Figure I could show her around tomorrow and perhaps introduce her to some of the single men who would be interested in marrying someone like Nancy."

"Sounds like a rather good idea. Well, I wish you the best of luck," the Mayor said as he went back into his office and sat back down at his desk. Dan sighed as he went further into the town hall and began to collect his things. Once everything was together, he left in a hurry to send that telegram and hopefully figure a plan out with Nancy.

PHOEBE'S EMOTIONS were ranging all over the place as she rode through the forest on her horse. She was leading the Indian children back to camp and the ride had been very quiet save for the natural sounds of the forest. In this silence, she was able to think about what she'd just seen and try to come to terms with all of it.

He's a cheater just like the last one, Phoebe would think to herself.

No, that can't be true. There has to be a reasonable explanation for all of this. Dan is a caring and loving man. He's not the type to sleep around with a bunch of women.

But then why did that woman show up out of nowhere? Was she really his mail-order-bride? No, that can't be true. He was as surprised as the rest of us that she just showed up out of nowhere.

What are they doing together now? Is she convincing him that she'd make a great wife for him? Had she lost her chance at love with Dan? Did she love Dan?

Phoebe was so lost in her thoughts that she'd hardly realized they'd made it to camp when her mare came to a stop even when she hadn't given the command. She looked around herself, seeing the other Indian ponies coming to a stop behind her as the kids eagerly dismounted and led the ponies over to the corral. She was relieved that they'd all made it back to camp without the children asking too many questions from her. But since they were back early, she knew she should expect to be questioned either by the parents or Brown Bear. A part of her even wondered if she should just head back to her cabin before anyone had a chance to approach her.

Thinking solitude was going to be the best option, Phoebe turned her horse from the camp and led him down the trail that would lead to her cabin. She already missed the sounds of the Indian camp as she wondered through the forest, still debating if her choice to leave was such a good idea. When she returned home, the cabin would be empty. She'd be alone for many hours until Edward came back from the mines. Perhaps some loneliness and solitude would do her some good as she contemplated what she was going to do next concerning Dan. She wouldn't even bother with showing up for book club tonight because she felt like she wouldn't be able to look him in the eye without having to deal with this anger deep inside of her.

As Phoebe made her way through the forest at a slow pace, she understood from where all these feelings of anger and betrayal came from. She'd experienced this all before from having dated a man she thought she was in love with. Phoebe scowled at herself, feeling upset because she should have known better.

"All men are the same," she mumbled to herself. "They keep secrets and see other women behind your back." She was doing her best to push back the tears that had been threatening to fall for some time. It was like reliving everything in Boston all over again. She'd allowed her heart to soften and had been ready to give it to another. Now, she was faced with the same dilemma. She had watched the man she'd prepared to give her heart to in the arms of another woman.

"How could I have been so stupid?" Phoebe said as she began to rub her hands on her thighs, feeling like her life was simply spiraling out of control. She needed to get her emotions under wraps once more and not let herself fall into such despair as last time. Even though she felt like she was reliving the past, she couldn't allow herself to feel like that ever again. Phoebe knew that now was the time that she'd need to guard her heart and never let it be exposed again.

Phoebe took her time dismounting from her mare once she reached the stables. The barn was pretty packed since all the miners left their horses in the barn while they worked, and two stable boys managed all the horses during that time. But wanting to tend to her own horse, Phoebe placed a lead rope to the horse to keep her still while Phoebe took her time taking the saddle off her horse and giving the mare a good brush. Afterwards, Phoebe led the mare into her stall and made sure she had plenty of feed before making her way to the cabin.

But as Phoebe crossed the area from the stables to the cabin, her heart froze in her chest as she saw Brown Bear standing by the front door with his Indian pony attached to a lead rope. The Indian chief was securing the pony to a nearby oak tree as Phoebe finished making her way over to him. When he turned back to her, he had a small bundle of wildflowers in his hand that he quickly handed to her once Phoebe was close enough.

"And what did I do to earn such a tender gift from an Indian chief?" Phoebe asked in Sioux.

"The Great Spirit told me that you could use some comfort. Also, the children told me what had happened once I noticed they were back early from school," Brown Bear explained.

"Would you care to come in, Brown Bear? I could fix us both a cup of tea."

"I think that would be pleasant, thank you." Phoebe then opened the cabin door and stepped inside. After she'd lit a few lanterns, she went about putting the kettle on the stove that she had to coax to life. While she worked, Brown Bear took a seat at their small table and simply watched her as though he was trying to understand how she felt.

"I know what the children have told me, and I can see that you are clearly upset. Why don't you tell me your side of the story?" Brown Bear offered once Phoebe finally came to sit down at the table with him. Phoebe was trying to gather her thoughts and decide how much she should share with the Indian chief.

"The lessons at the town hall were interrupted today by a strange woman I've never seen before. All I could do was just stand there and watch as she embraced Dan as though they were old friends. She said she'd come to be his mail-order-bride. However, Dan acted as though he'd never seen the woman before. That's when he dismissed everyone," Phoebe explained as she stared down at her cup of tea. She was trying to keep her emotions contained while she only stated the facts of the matter.

"It was Mathew who first taught me what mail-order-bride means. I would not have thought Dan would place an ad if you two were doing so well."

"I did not know he had placed an ad, either."

"But you would agree that things have been going well between you two? I would have guessed that perhaps Dan would be proposing." Phoebe couldn't help but smirk at the idea. Perhaps she would have grown excited at the idea earlier, but now she was certain she'd never allow herself to love again.

"I don't know what to believe anymore, Brown Bear. This isn't the first time I've been misled by a man who seemed to have pure intentions. I'm assuming Dan is just like the rest of them."

"I only hope you don't think I'm like the rest of them," Brown Bear said with a chuckle. Phoebe finally looked at him, knowing the Indian chief was honorable and virtuous through and through.

"Of course not. You've proven yourself worthy time and time again."

"And Dan has not?" Brown Bear was quick to ask. He was concerned about Phoebe and knew of her past from the conversations he'd had with her brother. Brown Bear didn't want to see Phoebe fall into a dark path once more. She'd livened up quite a lot since coming to Bear Creek, especially compared to the first time he'd met the James siblings. The last thing he wanted to see was a dark shadow come over Phoebe's heart once more.

"There was a moment when I thought Dan could truly be the one for me," Phoebe said as she looked down at her untouched tea. "But all I can think about right now is how badly I've been deceived once more."

"Phoebe, the only thing I fear is that your heart is the only thing that may be deceiving you. I may not know Dan very well, but I wouldn't have allowed the children to be taught by the man if I didn't feel like he had true and good intentions," Brown Bear said, hoping to convince Phoebe that her own past was the one thing that was making her feel like this.

"I appreciate your advice, Brown Bear, but I won't be able to make heads or tails of this situation right now," Phoebe said as she pushed herself to her feet and went to set her cup in the sink. She knew she wouldn't be drinking it any time soon. When she heard Brown Bear begin to chuckle, she turned around to see what was so funny.

"Forgive me. There are still some things I don't understand when you speak Sioux. I forget that the English saying, 'heads or tails' refers to a coin and not the parts of an animal," Brown Bear explained. Phoebe couldn't help but chuckle herself as she realized her error.

"Seems I am still learning," Phoebe reasoned.

"We are all still learning," Brown Bear said as he stood and finished his cup of tea before handing it back to Phoebe. "Sometimes we have to put our thoughts and fears aside to truly learn."

"Thank you for the flowers and your visit. I do appreciate it," Phoebe said, wanting to be alone now more than ever. She truly appreciated the Indian chief leaving camp simply to speak with her, but she knew that he would be needed back at camp soon enough.

"I hope you will come to camp for dinner. I was under the impression that Edward would already be there before too long.

It is Friday, after all, and you normally go into town for your book club." Phoebe opened the door for Brown Bear, thinking it might not hurt to join the others for the evening meal.

"I will consider it, thank you." Brown Bear grunted his approval before stepping through the threshold. Phoebe stood in the doorway and watched as the Indian chief untied the Indian pony and mounted the beast with swift movements. He nodded to her before leading the pony back along the trail to camp. Shutting the door, Phoebe went about tidying up the place the best she could if only to clear her mind from all the pressing thoughts that seemed to be bothering her today.

CHAPTER 9

*A*fter posting a small note on the door of the town hall explaining that the book club meeting would be canceled for that evening, Dan made his way towards the inn to have a final word with Nancy Tender. He was still in disbelief that things had gone the way they had today. It had been any other normal Friday with teaching his lessons to the children and working with Phoebe to teach the Indian children English. They'd all been doing so well that he thought his life was finally coming into a full balance. He even reasoned that perhaps in a few weeks he could propose to Phoebe once he was sure of her feelings for him. But with Nancy just appearing out of thin air, he wasn't sure what would happen between him and the woman he'd developed strong feelings for.

Dan crossed town and made it to the inn right as the dinner crowd started to file into the building. Miners were returning from the mountains and other locals came by to enjoy a good home-cooked meal. Dan enjoyed coming to the inn himself when he wasn't up to cooking, but tonight he just wanted to have a quick word with Nancy since he'd promised Mr. Tibet he'd be back as soon as he could. As Dan came into the inn, it didn't take him long to find Nancy sitting at a table in the dining room, surrounded by a small group of men as she chatted away excitedly.

"That's some woman there," Mr. Tibet said as he came to stand next to Dan as they both looked into the dining room together.

"Why do you say that, Mr. Tibet?" Dan asked.

"She slept like the dead for almost four hours before she finally woke to me telling her that there was food for her in the kitchen. She rose quickly and got dressed, met Mrs. Tibet and Mrs. Benning in the kitchen and hasn't stopped talking since. She's quick to tell everyone her sad story and can really attract a crowd, as you can see."

"Yeah, I can see that. I just don't know what to do about it."

"Well, she's been telling everyone not only the horrors she ran away from but how excited she is to be getting married to you." Dan sighed heavily at hearing this as he ran his hands through his hair, clearly frustrated.

"Thank you, Mr. Tibet, for your time and patience," Dan said as he looked to the older man. He simply nodded in return as he continued to greet the dinner guests and start taking their orders. He hoped that Dan would be able to figure things out with Nancy because he'd seen how close Dan and Phoebe had grown together over the last few weeks.

Dan took a steadying breath before entering the dining room. As soon as he did, Nancy seemed to become aware of him once more as she quickly stood and waved at him excitedly. As Dan glanced at the men around her, he saw how displeased they looked to see him. No doubt, Nancy had been talking to all of them about their upcoming marriage, but they'd stuck around because Nancy was an attractive redhead who obviously liked all the male appreciation.

"I wondered when I was going to get to see you once more," Nancy said as she came around the table and tried to embrace him. Dan was quick to capture her hands in his as he looked down at her with a stern expression in his eyes.

"I'm heading home for the night and wanted to let you know that in the morning I'll come by to show you the town and introduce you to the locals," Dan said as he let go of Nancy's hands, not wanting to have too much physical contact with her.

"Well, what am I supposed to do till then? Shouldn't we be planning out our wedding details?" she asked with pleading eyes.

"Nancy, I'm not planning on marrying you. I don't even know you. If you want to become a mail-order-bride, then that requires you actually writing the person you intend on marrying," Dan said as he tried to keep a tight hold on his temper.

"But I told you why I couldn't write you. And here I am. You should be grateful for everything I've done to get here," Nancy said, thinking that her idea of marrying Dan wasn't going as planned. She'd traveled awfully far to be his wife and the least he could do was try to accommodate her and her wishes.

"I understand why you left Indiana, and I don't blame you. But I'm not going to agree to marry you just because of your past. Now, Bear Creek is a wonderful town that I think you'll grow to love. Everyone does. And it seems you have company for the evening," Dan said as he gestured to the other men that were all seated around her table. "Why don't you enjoy a good meal and some company, then in the morning I can show you around."

"Well, I suppose that will be fine," Nancy grumbled as she lifted her gown and made her way back to her seat at the table. She sat down and looked up at Dan, a look of displeasure on her face. Having nothing more to say, Dan turned and quickly left the inn. He couldn't believe how anyone could just appear in someone's life and demand anything from them. He thought Nancy was crazy for thinking she could just expect him to marry her simply because he was in want of a wife. But since she'd had a very abusive father and probably had lived in fear for many years, he couldn't blame anyone for acting the way Nancy did in such circumstances. Perhaps she just needed a little bit of hope to convince her to leave. But now that she had made her way to Bear Creek, Dan only hoped that she'd find someone else she'd want to marry more than him.

Dan eventually collected his horse from the livery stables and made his way home by the light of the setting sun. Normally he would have been looking forward to being at the town hall with the other book club members. In a few weeks they'd be reading another novel and Dan was eager to share with the group what that title would be. He'd already ordered the books and hoped they'd arrive in time. But more than anything, he wanted to spend more time with Phoebe. He loved discussing literature with her because she always had great opinions about what the group was reading. He suspected it was because of her education as a young lady, but the other half of him just saw her as a very intelligent woman. Now, however, he was heading home alone without knowing when he'd get to see Phoebe next so he could try to explain the situation to her.

As Dan neared his cottage, he was surprised to see that there was a horse in his front lawn. As he drew closer, he saw that it was not just any horse, but an Indian pony. A part of him wondered if Phoebe had come to pay him a visit, but he knew her horse and that she rode side-saddle. It would be rather scandalous for a proper lady to ride bareback in a gown. But as Dan rode up to his stable, he saw sitting on his front stoop a very tall Indian that he recognized to be Brown Bear.

"I hope you haven't been waiting for me for too long," Dan said as he steered his mare over towards the front of the cottage, thinking he'd get her ready for the evening after he found out what the Indian chief wanted from him. Dan dismounted his horse and tied the reins to the hitching post as the Indian chief stood from where he was sitting, coming to stand almost eye to eye with Dan.

"No, I have not been here that long," Brown Bear said as he reached out his hand. Dan shook it, thinking that he'd never shaken the hand of an Indian before.

"What brings you to my home?" Dan asked, wondering if something had happened to the Indian children or Phoebe on their way back to camp. Dan tried hard to still his beating heart, hoping he wouldn't have any more bad news today.

"May I come in?" Brown Bear asked. "I wish to speak with you for a few minutes."

"Sure, that'd be fine," Dan replied, his worries and fears only seeming to grow stronger with each passing moment. He then unlocked his door and pushed open the door, allowing Brown Bear to enter first. He came into the cottage after him and set about lighting a few candles and coaxing the fire in the stove back to life.

"Can I make you any tea or coffee?" Dan asked, wanting to be a good host.

"No, no. I have had my fill for the day," Brown Bear said with a chuckle, thinking that Phoebe and Dan were very similar in that regard. "I wanted to come and talk to you about what happened today. I was surprised when I saw the Indian children arrive early from their lessons. Phoebe took the time to explain to me what had happened."

"How is Phoebe doing?" Dan asked point blankly as he stilled, desperate to know that she was okay. Brown Bear saw the concern in the young man's eyes and thought that it was a good sign that Dan actually cared about Phoebe.

"She is fine, I think. She seemed rather upset, if I am to be honest. It is why I came to talk to you, to hear your side of the story."

"Brown Bear, today has been an absolute nightmare," Dan admitted as he slumped down into a chair at the small table and indicated for Brown Bear to join him. The Indian chief sat in the chair across from him, feeling equally as concerned about Dan as he did about Phoebe. He waited patiently, wanting to hear what the man had to say.

"This woman, Nancy, just showed up at the town hall, completely interrupting the lessons for the day. She said she came to Bear Creek to be my mail-order-bride, but I had never met the woman before nor exchanged any letters with her. I had no idea she was just going to show up and practically demand that we marry right away."

"That must have been quite surprising and frustrating," Brown Bear commented as he watched Dan closely, trying to discern for himself whether or not the teacher was lying to him at all. He was very good at telling whether or not a man was being truthful to him as he spoke.

"I've never been more stressed out in my life," Dan said as he ran his fingers through his hair once more, thinking he'd better get a haircut soon. "I never like sending the children home early, but I couldn't see any other way around it. Nancy was making such a spectacle that I knew it was in their best interest. And with Nancy telling everyone she can that we're getting married, I'm afraid this stranger has ruined my reputation as well."

"What do you think would possess a woman to leave her home and expect a stranger to marry her?" Brown Bear asked. This is when Dan took the time to tell the Indian chief Nancy's history and all that she'd run away from.

"Ah, I see now. The woman is driven by fear and desperation. She desires a husband who will actually take proper care of her and thought someone like you would be the one to do that," Brown Bear said once Dan had finished explaining. "You are a very kind and generous man. It would be easy for a woman like Nancy to take advantage of you."

"Well, tomorrow morning I'm going to introduce her to other people in town. I'm hoping she can find someone else she would rather marry. I've already tried to make it clear to her that I will not marry her just because she's single and willing. In fact, I've already sent a telegram to the newspapers in the East to cancel my ad. I don't think I want to try for a mail-order-bride anymore."

"And what about Phoebe? What plans do you have towards her?" Brown Bear asked, wanting to know for a surety how the schoolteacher felt about the young woman.

"I want to talk to her and tell her what happened. I can't imagine what she must be thinking about me right now, but I hope that once she hears the truth that she won't be so upset about the situation. I really like Phoebe and I'm afraid that Nancy has ruined any chances I had with her."

"I don't think they are ruined, Dan, but I agree that Phoebe is upset. I hope that Phoebe will see reason once you two finally talk about what happened today. But I fear her heart is very broken from her life in Boston. It might take some time to get her to open up to you once more," Brown Bear advised. "But I don't think all hope is lost."

"You are very considerate to be looking after Phoebe since

she isn't a part of your tribe," Dan said, wondering what Phoebe must have said to the Indian chief to warrant a personal visit.

"I consider all a part of my tribe, Dan. Edward and Phoebe James are at the camp so often that I just consider them one of my own. And after watching Phoebe become used to Bear Creek for the last few years, I think it would do her some good to finally find someone she can love and receive love in return."

"You really think I could be that person for Phoebe?" Dan asked, feeling a surge of excitement course through him as he listened to Brown Bear speak.

"I've seen how happy she's been since she's started taking the Indian children to town each day for their lessons. I like to think that is because of you. I also see the way you two act around one another in camp. I would be a liar if I didn't say that you two have a good chance to be together." Dan let out a shaky breath as he considered his words. He liked the reassurance he was getting from Brown Bear that he and Phoebe were seen as a good match by someone else. Dan just hoped that it could all be true.

"I appreciate you taking the time to come all the way out here to talk with me," Dan eventually said. "I'm glad to hear that Phoebe and the children made it back to camp without any issue. Sometimes I really worry about them."

"The children are stronger than they appear. Especially the older ones. They have all been trained from a young age to hunt and defend themselves from the predators of the forest."

"Forgive me, Brown Bear, but when I see them, I simply see children."

"Understandable. I pray that neither one of us will ever have to see their training in action till they are much older," Brown Bear said as he stood from the table. "I must make my way back to camp for the evening meal. Would you care to join me?"

"Thank you for the offer, but I think I need some time by myself to think and make a plan for tomorrow," Dan explained as he stood as well and escorted the Indian chief to the front door once more.

"You are a wise man for taking the time to plan out your next action. You remind me of a wise warrior preparing for battle in the morning," Brown Bear said as he stepped out the front door that Dan held open for him.

"Perhaps it will be like a battle in the morning, but one I must win with my mind instead of my hands," Dan reasoned, liking the analogy that Brown Bear had used.

"Well, I look forward to hearing how the battle went," Brown Bear said as he leaped onto the back of his Indian pony with much grace and ease. Dan wasn't sure if he could ever learn to do something like that even though he was quite tall. Even though Brown Bear was growing older in age, he still moved like one of his young Indian braves.

Dan waved from the open door as Brown Bear nodded towards him before taking off into the night. He wasn't sure how the Indian chief did it, traveling so far by night. But Dan figured that he was simply used to it or trained from a young age to venture through the forest at night. Once he shut the door, Dan turned his mind to his own evening meal and what he was going to do in the morning with Nancy to convince her that not only was Bear Creek a decent place to live, that there were plenty of other single men for her to choose from. Dan simply had to find a way out of this mess so he could finally take the time to tell Phoebe how he truly cared for her.

WHEN THE SUN had started to set, Phoebe made her way to camp.

There was no point making dinner when her brother would already be at camp and there was always plenty enough to eat during the evening meals. Though the setting sun sent very little light through the forest canopy, both her and her mare knew the trail by heart. Phoebe rode through the forest, her heart and mind at war with one another. She tried to think about Brown Bear's words of advice but kept thinking about her terrible experience with love when she lived in Boston.

As she crossed through the tree line surrounding the camp, Phoebe had a difficult time focusing on herself. After she let her mare loose with the other Indian ponies, she made her way to the central fire pit where everyone was milling about in preparation for dinner. She smiled and said hello to the many familiar faces, and once she reached where she was going, she fell in line with the other maidens in helping prepare the meal. With a task to do and friendly women to talk with, it was easy to lose herself in the work and not think any more about her own personal issues.

While Phoebe worked on grinding corn that would be mixed with water to create almost a pancake, she caught sight of her brother across the fire pit. The central fire was pretty low since the days and nights were still pretty warm. It was only built up because meat needed to be cooked. And since the fire was pretty low, Phoebe could easily see across the central ring to see her brother talking with an Indian maiden. She watched the two closely and was surprised when he leaned down and placed a kiss on her cheek. She hadn't heard her brother say anything about having feelings for one of the maidens, but it seemed that everyone knew but her since the women around her started to comment on their intimate presence together.

"Seems there will be a wedding before winter," one of the older women said, giving Phoebe a wink.

"Morning Sun seems very attached to the white man. I wonder how her parents feel about the couple?" said another.

"Remember, Edward James is half-Indian. Surely the parents won't mind."

"But he was raised white and only later accepted his Indian heritage. It would be better for Morning Sun to marry a true Indian. Surely the young girl won't like living the way of the white people?"

"Do you really think Edward would make her live in that cabin? Maybe Edward would instead move to this camp since he spends so much time here?"

"Well, I'm not sure what they'll decide, but it all depends on her father agreeing to the match first."

As Phoebe listened, she was concerned about her brother. If he was falling in love with the maiden, did he understand what all would be at stake? He was very much a white settler by all standards that the Indians saw, and though most accepted Edward and Phoebe as good friends of the tribe, would this type of marriage really strain that relationship? It seemed to be one more thing for Phoebe to worry about. The last thing she wanted was to lose her friends inside the Indian tribe all because Edward couldn't win over his lover's father. Phoebe dearly hoped that if Edward did want to marry Morning Sun that everything would go well, and people would be accepting of their union. And if Edward did move to live with the Indians after his marriage, what would become of her? Would she have to live at camp as well? Though she spent a good bit of her time amongst the Indians, she still liked the comforts of the cabin.

When the sun had finally set, the tribe gathered around the central fire pit. The fire was built up to shed more light around the surrounding area so everyone could see as food was passed around. Phoebe helped the women pass along the food, and once everyone seemed to have their share, Phoebe gathered her own plate of corncakes and venison stew and found a place to sit alone. She wasn't really in the mood for talking with anyone as she seemed to be consumed by her thoughts. However, she did notice when Brown Bear came riding into camp. It made her wonder where he'd been all this time.

"Shouldn't you be at your book club?" someone asked, causing Phoebe to look up at the person who had addressed her. She noticed her brother standing over her then and figured he'd finally noticed her amongst all the others.

"I'm not going tonight," Phoebe replied as Edward settled into a spot next to her.

"How come?" he asked, taking her empty plate and passing it along to be collected by the maidens. They'd then take all the dirty dishes to be washed. Phoebe knew she should probably join them to help out, but it seemed her brother wanted her undivided attention.

"It was a very stressful day and I thought it would be nice to have a relaxing evening," Phoebe said, not wanting to explain to one more person why she was in a sore mood.

"By sitting here by yourself? Come on, Phoebe. You can tell me anything," Edward said as he lowered his voice. After a few more minutes, he took her by the chin and forced her to look at him as she tried to look away to play with blades of grass between her fingers. Eventually, Phoebe gave in and told her brother everything that had happened today. Afterwards, they sat in silence for a few minutes. During that time, she worried what Edward's reaction was going to be.

"It's hard justifying me beating the man to a pulp if you're not sure if he was cheating on you this whole time or not," Edward said after a while. "I don't mind doing the work to teach that man a lesson, but it seems like you don't have all the facts just yet."

"That's part of the issue, Edward. It's such a strange circumstance that I don't know what to think. I know it angers me to think I feel for a man who just used me in the end. I was really starting to develop feelings for Dan, and then something like this happens. I fear that I'm just going to repeat my past." Phoebe felt like she was rambling, but a part of her thought that it was good to talk to the person she trusted the most with what she was feeling.

"I'm not going to allow a man to hurt you like you were, Phoebe," Edward said as he took her hand. "And though I don't know much about Dan, he never came across to me as the type of man who would be capable of being with two women at once."

"And that's what I thought about Gavin at one point myself," Phoebe said as she removed her hand from Edward's grasp, feeling angry all over again. "I trusted that man with my life and gave him something I can never take back. And once he had it, he tossed me to the side like I was trash."

"And do you really think Dan would be capable of something like that?" Edward pressed. He was worried about his sister because she'd been working so hard to put her past behind her. But after that incident, it felt to Edward as though they were reliving that entire situation because of what had happened today.

"I don't know, Edward, I simply don't know. How can I determine what is truth and what is not when I've been lied to so badly in the past?" Phoebe said as she wrapped her arms around her legs and rested her head on her knees. "I think I should just go back to the cabin and go to bed."

"There's no point in sulking, Phoebe. You simply need to go talk to Dan about what really happened today," Edward said as he placed his hand on Phoebe's shoulder, trying to comfort her the best he could.

"I'm not going to go talk to him tonight, and I doubt I'll make it into town tomorrow. So why don't you tell me what's going on between you and Morning Sun," Phoebe said, hoping to turn the conversation back around on him. Edward smirked as he withdrew his hand and looked across the way to where Morning Sun was sitting with her family. Their eyes locked for just a moment, and in that moment his heart roared for her.

"I'm sure it's not a secret to anyone that I have strong feelings about her," Edward said. "I simply don't know how to go about proposing to her. I doubt she'd live in the cabin with us since it's such a small space, and I don't know if I'd be willing to move here at camp. That would leave you all alone in the cabin and I don't really like the idea of that."

"I'm guessing you've given this great consideration," Phoebe reasoned. "Do you know how her parents feel about you? What are you willing to offer in return for Morning Star? It's not like you have ponies or hunting trophies to offer her father."

"Yeah, I know. I've been thinking a lot about it and I'm always trying to think of a way to make this relationship work. I think I've fallen in love with Morning Star and I want to always be with her." Phoebe was surprised to hear this. She'd known that her brother had previous relationships before, but he'd never spoken about another woman like this.

"I'm happy for you, Edward. If there is anything I can do to help your situation, please let me know," Phoebe said, trying her best to reassure her brother. He'd been there for her when she'd needed someone desperately to rescue her from a dire situation. She'd give anything to help him in return for all that he'd done for her.

"Thank you, Phoebe. That truly means a lot to me," Edward

said after a while. "Well, let's get home. The dawn waits for no man." Edward then helped Phoebe to her feet, thinking it was time for them to head home and get ready for the night. Things had been progressing nicely in the mines and he felt like he should be throwing himself into his work instead of worrying about what was going to happen between him and Morning Sun. He felt in his heart that he was destined to be with her, but he wasn't sure how that would happen. For now, he was content in knowing that she returned his feelings.

After saying goodnight to their friends, Phoebe and Edward made their way back through the forest as night set in. Phoebe felt safe with her brother nearby as her mare followed closely behind the gelding. There was something about the silence of the night that comforted Phoebe. It was calming to know that the night required nothing of her and only allowed her to pass through without taking anything in return. The day demanded she move and take action while the night would simply let her be.

CHAPTER 10

*D*an was up early the next morning, anxious to get the day over with. He was going to do his best to convince Nancy he wasn't her ideal husband. Therefore, he didn't comb his hair after he got out of bed, he put on his work jeans, the ones he used when he was mucking his mare's stall or when he tended to his garden. And lastly, he wore a very old western shirt that was missing a few buttons and didn't smell the greatest. As Dan looked himself over in the mirror, he was sure that he'd have Nancy running for the hills upon seeing him. Though, he hoped he didn't run into Phoebe looking like this.

After a quick breakfast, Dan headed into town with butter-flies in his stomach. He knew he looked foolish and those who knew him best would more than likely think that something was very wrong with him. He felt a little embarrassed but was certain his plan would work. Later, he was sure he'd look back on this memory and laugh heartily to himself. But till later, he was feeling a bit of trepidation as he rode into town.

"Morning, Mr. Mavis!" called one of the stable hands as he rode into the livery stables. The man looked at him and did a double take. "You doing alright?" Dan had to do his best not to laugh as he dismounted and handed the reins over to the man.

"I'm right as rain," Dan said with a nod before he made his way out of the barn. He hurried towards the inn, hoping that Nancy was up and ready to have a proper tour of the town. He had a few businessmen in mind that he wanted to introduce to Nancy with the hope of showing her that the town was full of single men and that he wasn't the best candidate for a husband.

As Dan stepped into the inn, he felt his palms start to grow damp from nervousness. He hoped that Nancy was already up and waiting for him so he could get this little situation over with. Dan also didn't want to remain in this silly get-up longer than he needed to. As he walked through the lobby of the inn, he met Mr. Tibet just as he was coming out of the kitchen. The older man stopped dead in his tracks and simply stared at Dan for a moment as though he wasn't sure what he was seeing.

"Have you gone mad, Mr. Mavis?" Mr. Tibet asked after a moment.

"No, Mr. Tibet. Just playing a little pretend is all," Dan replied. He thought his words were just in time as Nancy came walking out of the kitchen with Mrs. Benning right behind her. The married woman had grown round with child and she seemed to be doing her best to keep up with Nancy as the young woman continued to chatter on. But once Nancy caught sight of Dan, she immediately stopped talking and simply stared at him. She appeared to have the same reaction as Mr. Tibet had upon first seeing him.

"Well, good morning, Dan," she eventually said as she walked up to him. She was wearing a pretty blue gown that she was sure other men would find attractive on her. Her curly red hair had been pinned up into a stylish updo, and perhaps if things hadn't gotten off on such bad footing, he'd even consider Nancy for her beauty alone. Though, his heart was still dead set on Phoebe.

"Good morning, Nancy. I hope you're ready for that tour of the town," Dan said in his best country accent. The three of them looked at Dan strangely. Mrs. Benning started shaking her head as she turned and returned to the kitchen, closely followed by Mr. Tibet who simply shrugged his shoulders.

"Why yes, Mr. Mavis. I think that would be lovely," Nancy said in an uneasy voice. Dan watched as her eyes moved from his toes to his head, taking in his full attire. He was praying that Nancy would fall for his act and start to reconsider him for a husband. He offered his arm out to her and she eventually took it, placing her hand lightly around his elbow as he led her out of the inn. Dan looked down at her and noticed the way she crinkled her nose, more than likely getting a whiff of his smelly shirt.

"Bear Creek was founded two generations ago when the mine was first discovered. It's been a miner's town through and through, and still is today," Dan explained, doing his best to keep up his accent and dumb down his words. "The town has a handful of businesses that I think you'd be interested in seeing. Let's go over and check out the butcher, Curtis Denver."

"I've never been real fond of butcher shops," Nancy admitted as Dan led her through the town.

"Ah, don't worry. Curtis doesn't bite," Dan said with a chuckle. But the moment they stepped onto the front porch of the shop, Nancy dropped her hand from his.

"It's the smell that always gets me," she admitted. "I'm just happy to know there is a butcher, but I'm not quite fond of going in." Dan wasn't a cruel man and wouldn't want to put her through any discomfort. After all, he wanted her to like Bear Creek and truly find a husband after all she'd been through.

"Alright then. Let me show you the general store," Dan said as he led her over in that direction. "Right here is the jail and the Sheriff's Office. Deputy Tanner is probably in the office if you'd like to meet him."

"I'm more curious about the general store," Nancy said. "I used to work at a store and would be interested in learning if the owner might need any help."

"You never know. Mr. and Mrs. Fry are getting along in their years and might need some assistance. Mrs. Fry is a seamstress if you need any of your clothes repaired."

"Oh, do you think she could help me make a wedding dress?" Nancy asked, her eyes lighting up for the first time that day. Dan didn't want to reply to that question, but he also didn't want to be blatantly rude.

"You could always ask her," Dan suggested.

"Alright, let's get moving," Nancy said as she took his elbow and started leading him towards the store in a hurry. He groaned inside, wishing she wasn't so focused on this wedding business.

Inside the store, Dan did his best to create space between him and Nancy. He introduced her to Mr. and Mrs. Fry and then went up and down the aisles as though he was shopping. Really, he just needed a moment to himself to collect his thoughts. Curtis and Tanner were two of the most prominent single men in town. There were plenty of miners, but they'd all be up in the mountains this time of day. And Dan didn't really have all that much time to take Nancy out of town to meet some of the single men that either worked as ranch hands or owned farms. There was only one other person he knew of that might be available.

"Nancy, I hate to interrupt," Dan said as he came up to the counter where Nancy was chatting away with Mrs. Fry. "But I'm going to pop into the barber shop two doors down and get a haircut by Mitchel Franks. Why don't you meet me there when you're done?"

"Sure thing, Dan," Nancy said with a bright smile before she began talking with Mrs. Fry once more. The two seemed to be getting along mighty fine, but as Dan glanced at Mr. Fry, the man was observing him closely as though he was trying to figure Dan out. Dan simply waved at the man before he left the general store and walked down the boardwalk to the barbershop. As he entered, he was glad he was the only one in need of a haircut that day.

"Dear Lord, Dan. Looks like you need something more than just a haircut. I got tubs in the back if you need a bath because you sure smell like you do," Mitchel Franks said as he rose from his barber's chair.

"I know I must look like a fool, but there is a reason to my madness," Dan said. "Now, how about a haircut?"

"Suit yourself," Mitchel replied as he motioned towards the chair. For such a muscular guy, Mitchel was careful and precise with his cutting shears. As Dan settled into the chair and tipped his head back over the edge, Mitchel began combing his hair with a wet comb to try to tame his hair enough to where he could cut it properly.

"You look like you just rolled out of bed and didn't bother doing anything with your hair," Mitchel said as he shook his head.

"That was kind of the idea," Dan admitted. "I'll have to tell you the whole story one day."

Just then, Nancy came walking into the barbershop in a hurry. She was talking excitedly once more, something about a possible job offer, when she stopped suddenly and came into eye contact with Mitchel. Dan smiled as he watched the exchange between the two, seeing how both of them seemed interested in the other. Dan watched Mitchel's eyes as he looked over Nancy, his mouth parting slightly as he lowered his cutting shears from Dan's head. As Dan looked back at Nancy, he saw her smooth down her dress as a small smile came onto her face as though she'd suddenly become very shy.

"Mitchel, I'd like to introduce you to Nancy Tender. She arrived in Bear Creek yesterday," Dan said when silence continued on between them. His words seemed to snap them both out of whatever deep thoughts they were having about one another and Nancy quickly looked to her feet, seeming to be at a loss for words.

"It's a pleasure to make your acquaintance," Mitchel said as he extended his free hand towards her. When she allowed him to take her hand, Dan felt a leap of joy surge through him as Mitchel turned her hand upside down and kissed her knuckles like a true gentleman. Dan could see the deep blush that settled over Nancy's face as her eyes widened suddenly at the contact of his lips on her hand.

"The pleasure is all mine," Nancy replied as she reclaimed her hand.

"Tell me about your visit with Mrs. Fry," Dan suggested as Mitchel returned to cutting his hair. Nancy focused on him then, seeming to notice him for the first time.

"Mrs. Fry needs some help keeping the store tidy and with some mending. I can do both and offered to help her and Mr. Fry out during the day or whenever they really need me. And, they're willing to pay me decently enough."

"That's wonderful news. Don't you think, Mitchel?" Dan said, trying to include the barber in on the conversation.

"I think that's mighty fine considering you just arrived yesterday. What brought you to Bear Creek anyways?" Mitchel asked. Nancy looked at Dan for a moment and tried to think of the best way to explain herself to a man she was finding very handsome and smelled wonderful, compared to Dan.

"I've been wanting to leave my home in Indiana for a long time because I had a very abusive father. I got wind of Bear Creek and never looked back. Traveled for weeks on my own to finally get here. And so far, I'm liking what I see," Nancy explained, her eyes traveling up and down Mitchel's muscular frame. She was thinking he had to be extremely strong with those types of muscles, yet he cut Dan's hair as though he was the gentlest creature on earth.

"I'm sorry to hear about your father. My dad wasn't the greatest, either. When I told him I was done roping cattle and wanted to cut hair for a living, he threw me out of my childhood home. I made my way to Bear Creek when I heard there wasn't someone here to cut hair and do shavings. Been here for about five years now." Dan hadn't ever heard Mitchel's story before and thought he was sure learning a lot from the man.

"Seems we have a lot in common then," Nancy said softly as she took a few steps forward as though she wanted to get a better look at Mitchel. He didn't seem to mind as he gave her a kind smile.

"You're all done, Mr. Mavis," Mitchel said as he brushed Dan's shoulders with his horsehair brush with a wooden handle. Dan got up from the chair and paid the man before making his way to the door.

"You needing that tour of the town still?" Dan asked Nancy.

"No, you go on along now. I think Mitchel can help me if I need anything," Nancy said as she continued to look at the barber with a bright smile on her face.

"Don't worry, Dan. I'll make sure she gets where she needs to go," Mitchel spoke up then.

"Much obliged," Dan said as he then turned from them and made his way out of the shop. As the door closed behind him, Dan took a nice long, deep breath. He was pleased with himself that his plan had gone perfectly well, and that Nancy had taken a fascination with someone else. He was certain it had a lot to do with Dan's current outfit and the way he looked, along with the way he was talking. Dan was also convinced that Mitchel was a good match for Nancy because they seemed to share a similar upbringing. As Dan walked away from the barbershop and towards the livery stables so he could return home and change, he only hoped that Nancy and Mitchel would soon be an official couple.

PHOEBE WASN'T TOO happy with having to head into town that morning. Edward had asked her to go in his place to meet with the Mayor to give the man an update on the mines. Part of Edward's work ethic was to keep a good reputation with the local authorities. He was well situated with Brown Bear, but since he rarely went to town, he needed to make appointments with Mr. Franklin to keep up appearances. But with him trying to figure out a way to marry Morning Sun, he'd asked Phoebe to go in his place to give the Mayor the latest reports on the mine. Knowing she'd promised Edward to help him in any way that she could, she'd agreed to do this for her brother even though she dreaded the thought of running into Dan.

With it being Saturday, Phoebe knew that it was a high possibility that she'd run into Dan at the town hall. He often tutored adults on the weekends, helping them improve their basic reading and writing skills. Since most young men and woman didn't make it past the eighth grade before they were needed more at home to help out either on the family farm or ranch, that meant most adults in Bear Creek only had a very basic and minimum education.

It made Phoebe grateful for the unlimited amounts of education she'd received, to include the learning of many modern languages with French being her favorite. It's probably why she learned Sioux so easily because she was already accustomed to learning different languages since she was a child. All of her education had been designed to make her more desirable as a wife to the wealthy elite of Boston society. But now that she was living in a remote country town, she tried to use her education to help others.

Once Phoebe made it out of the forest and down most of the mountain, she urged her mare into a faster pace. She was hoping to make this a quick trip to town and wasn't even going to stop at the general store. She'd do that in a few days since she'd be attending the sermon at the town hall, accompanied by her brother. Today she simply wanted to deliver the reports to the Mayor and answer any of his questions before making her way back up the mountain. The very idea of running into Dan with the other woman's arm on his made her skin crawl. All sorts of emotions were swimming in Phoebe's mind as she finally made it to the livery stables and handed over the reins to her mare.

"I shouldn't be too long," Phoebe said to the stable boy.

"Don't worry, Miss James. I'll make sure your mare is ready for you when you get back. It must be some journey to travel all the way from the mines into town."

"It's not difficult when the views are so lovely," Phoebe replied with a dip of her head. Some habits were just hard to break she realized as she left the barn with her leather satchel over her shoulder. Inside were all the handwritten documents the Mayor would be expecting. They included not only a list of all the miners Edward had hired, but also the production levels of the mines and what types of things they were currently finding. Also, Edward kept a detailed map of the tunnels that were currently being dug out in order to show that he was making sure to keep a safe distance away from the Indian camp and also their prominent hunting grounds. Phoebe knew that these were important papers and she felt proud in a sense to be handling this business for her brother. It wasn't the sort of thing her father would ever let her do, and if she'd married Gavin after all, she was certain he'd keep her at home instead of allowing her to join him at the office like he once promised.

Pushing those dreaded thoughts out of her mind, Phoebe crossed the main road leading up through town, careful to avoid any horse riders or wagons coming through. Phoebe had also learned to watch where she was stepping because the streets weren't often cleaned up after all the horses. The livery stable workers tried to do a good job, but they couldn't be everywhere at once. When Phoebe had successfully crossed the road, she looked up the stairs at the town hall and said a silent prayer that she wouldn't run into Dan that morning. But as she took the stairs up to the door, she could clearly hear familiar voices on the other side.

"My goodness, Mr. Mavis. Weren't you looking like a hot mess this morning?" the Mayor said, stopping Dan outside his office when Dan was in the process of getting ready for his tutoring lesson with Mr. Fry. They'd been practicing for weeks on his readability skills and he'd really improved.

"There was a reason for my frantic state of dress," Dan said with a sigh. "I think my plan worked. The moment Nancy caught sight of me and then smelled me, she seemed eager to find someone else. My bet is that she and Mitchel are hitting it off right away."

"Really? Your plan actually worked?" Mr. Franklin asked as he furrowed his brows together in disbelief.

"It seems so. Nancy just wanted someone to marry and protect her. Mitchel is a big, strong guy but can be as gentle as a lamb when cutting hair. Seems like a match made in heaven," Dan said with a chuckle.

"Your mop of hair does look a lot better than it did yesterday," the Mayor reasoned as he took in his appearance. Dan had gone home, bathed, and dressed in his normal teaching clothes. He always tried to look professional even though he didn't own a large variety of clothes. He simply wore what was in the best condition whether that was slacks or jeans, a western shirt or a cotton-pressed shirt with his suit jacket.

"Why thank you, Mr. Franklin."

"So, have you had a chance to talk to Phoebe yet about the whole misunderstanding?"

"I haven't yet, but I hope to soon. She deserves an explanation," Dan admitted.

"You two seem perfect for each other, just like Nancy appears to be perfect for Mitchel. I hope the actions of one person hasn't deeply affected what you and Miss James seem to have."

"I sure hope so, too. Nancy is certainly not the type of wife I want," Dan said just as the front door opened. They looked to see who was coming in as Dan assumed that Mr. Fry had shown up for their lesson. But when he saw Phoebe entering, his heart leaped for joy as his body cringed. Had she overheard their conversation at all, he wondered.

"Good morning, Miss James. What a pleasant surprise when I

was expecting your brother about this time," Mr. Franklin said with a smile, looking between Dan and Phoebe as he thought this was a very suspicious coincidental situation.

"My brother has some other pressing matters that he must attend to. I agreed to come in his place to deliver the bi-monthly reports and answer any questions you might have," Phoebe replied. She looked at Dan briefly, noticing he'd gotten a haircut. She thought the style looked nice on him, but it only made her wonder if he'd freshened up his look for the other woman.

"Well, that is mighty kind of you. Your brother is lucky to have such a smart sister who can help him with the business side of things. If it wasn't for Mr. and Mrs. Tibet helping me manage the boarding house, I wouldn't really know much of what I was doing. Even hired a front desk attendant to take care of things so I didn't have to be over there all the time."

"It's nice to live in such a supportive community," Dan added, wanting a chance to find a footing in the conversation so perhaps he could talk to Phoebe real quick.

"I absolutely agree with you, Dan. In fact, you should tell Miss James how you helped that poor girl that seemed to come into town like a tornado find a suitable match," Mr. Franklin said in hopes of helping Dan out with his little problem with Phoebe. Dan looked at the Mayor and wished he'd kept his mouth shut till he could have a private moment with Phoebe.

"Well, yeah. I helped Miss Nancy Tender meet some other people in town once I explained I wasn't going to marry a stranger. Took a little convincing, but she and Mitchel seem to have really hit things off," Dan explained as he looked in Phoebe's eyes, pleading with her to believe him.

"I think if you didn't want a wife, Mr. Mavis, you shouldn't have advertised for one," Phoebe said, her bitterness getting the best of her.

"With so few eligible young ladies in our small town, I really didn't have any other option. I do want a wife someday, but not with a complete stranger. I'd really like to settle down with a woman I can respect and who can go toe-to-toe with me with different discussions. And believe me when I say it's hard meeting women with my same level in intelligence," Dan said, doing his best to defend himself and his decision to place a mail-order-bride ad. "But after what happened with Miss Tender, I telegrammed the newspaper yesterday to have my ad canceled right away. I don't want any other woman coming to town thinking they can just expect me to marry them because I placed an ad. Though, I will say, I'm happy for Mitchel if things do work out."

Phoebe thought about what he said for a moment, thinking it was rather logical. And as she thought more about the time they'd been spending together, she thought Dan must really fancy her because she knew she possessed a higher intelligence than most women of her age simply because of her upbringing. It made Phoebe curious about how he truly felt about her since she seemed to be the perfect woman for him. But she also thought that Dan should have said something earlier about him having placed a mail-order-bride ad since that was serious business.

"I wish you success in finding your ideal woman, Mr. Mavis. Perhaps you should be clearer with your intentions in the future," Phoebe said before walking into the Mayor's office. Dan watched her go, noticing the stiffness in her shoulders. He had to admit that she looked beautiful as ever with her long brown hair flowing down her back, the top tied back just a bit to allow her ease to work and see. She might be upset with him, but his heart still beat strong for her.

Dan and Mr. Franklin exchanged a sympathetic look. Dan was thankful that Mr. Franklin had tried to help, and the Mayor hoped that their relationship could be mended. The Mayor closed the office door just as Mr. Fry was coming into the town hall at a slow pace. He was getting older in years and Dan was certain that the store owner didn't enjoy taking the stairs. Dan smiled at the older man as he greeted him, shaking his hand, and then led him to the front of the town hall where they'd use his desk to continue their reading lessons.

"Mr. Mavis. Are you going to tell me why you looked so strange this morning?" Mr. Fry asked as he settled down into his chair and set his writing tablet on the desk. Ever since Mr. Mavis had come into his shop with that strange woman, he couldn't stop thinking about the encounter. Though he'd learned that Miss Tender was a very nice lady that was eager to help around the store, it didn't quite explain Dan's appearance.

"There is a reason for it, Mr. Fry, but that will have to be a story for another day," Dan said with a chuckle. He knew how much Mr. Fry liked to gossip and didn't particularly like the idea of his personal issues being talked about throughout town.

"If you say so, young man," Mr. Fry said as he turned his attention to the sentences that Dan wanted him to write. First Dan would write them, then Mr. Fry would have to read the sentence out loud before taking his try at writing them himself. Mr. Fry knew how important it was that he keep track of all his store records, but he wouldn't be able to do the best job he could if he didn't get a little help with his writing ability.

When the door to the Mayor's office opened, Dan couldn't help but look up while Mr. Fry was in the middle of writing his sentence on his tablet with a small piece of chalk. Dan watched as Mr. Franklin bid Phoebe goodbye before disappearing back into his office. Then, Phoebe turned and looked at him, making Dan wish he could speak privately with her one more time. He didn't like the idea of Phoebe being upset with him or thinking he was someone he wasn't. She simply looked at him for a moment before turning and leaving the town hall. Dan knew that if he wasn't in the middle of a lesson with Mr. Fry, he'd run after her and make her see reason. Dan only hoped that his chance with Phoebe wasn't completely over with.

CHAPTER 11

*T*he town was congested the next morning as Pastor Munster made his monthly trip to Bear Creek to provide a sermon and perform any other ceremonies that needed to take place. All the town's people attended the sermon, and many of the families that lived outside of town took the day off to enjoy Pastor Munster's passionate sermons that always left you feeling whole and at peace. A large crowd always came together for these monthly sermons, and many of the town's people wished that Pastor Munster could make Bear Creek his permanent residence. But with the territory of Montana having few, and far between, religious leaders, Pastor Munster explained that he had a job to do and that was speaking to all of God's people as often as he could.

Dan stood amongst the crowd as everyone took their time stepping in through the doors of the town hall where Pastor Munster stood greeting everyone. He was a very tall man with broad shoulders as though he was more fitting to be a lumber jack. And though his frame was slightly intimidating, it was the bright smile on his face that always made a person feel at ease around him. Dan had dressed in his nicest Sunday dress, a pair of black slacks and his black vest buttoned over a white muslin shirt. He felt at ease as he waited for his turn to go through the door and greet the pastor, but that all changed when he saw a bundle of bright red hair coming his way through the crowd.

"Oh, Dan! There you are. How are you doing today?" Nancy asked as she made her way over to him. Dan gave an apologetic look to the couple she'd just crossed in front of to reach him because they clearly appeared put off that Nancy had just dashed in front of them as though they didn't exist.

"I'm fine, thank you," Dan said carefully, wondering what Nancy might be up to today and what intentions she had towards him.

"Good, glad to hear. Well, I don't mean to break your heart but I'm not certain we can get married. Things have been going great between Mitchel and me," she said with a shy smile on her face.

"I'm truly glad to hear this, Miss Tender. Trust me when I say my feelings are not hurt in the least," Dan reassured her.

"Oh, good! I was so nervous to tell you, but you're truly a good man, Dan. I really hope you find your special someone one day, like I have found mine." Dan thought that was the nicest and most reasonable thing Nancy had said to him yet. "Well, I better get back to Mitchel before he goes inside without me. I can't wait to meet the pastor who will probably be marrying us." Nancy then turned and hurried off through the crowd once more, her excitement apparent. When she reached Mitchel's side once more, they looped arms together and proceeded inside. From where Dan was standing, he thought that he could see that Nancy and Mitchel were truly happy together.

"Seems like the woman really hit it off with another man,"

came a soft female voice from beside him. Dan turned to look who had come up behind him and was pleasantly surprised to see Phoebe standing there with her arm resting on her brother's. Dan looked up at Edward and met a hard expression that he often saw on the Indian braves the few times he'd been to camp.

"Yes, Miss Tender and Mr. Franks seem to have become quite a pair in the short amount of time that the woman has been in town. I'm just glad she found what she came to Bear Creek looking for," Dan said as he looked back at Phoebe. She was radiant in the purple silk gown with short sleeves. White lace trimmed the neckline of the gown and it was very apparent to Dan that at one point the James siblings were rather wealthy.

"Phoebe told me of the strange occurrence. I did not take you for a man who played with women's hearts," Edward spoke up in a cold tone.

"That is because I don't, Mr. James. I did place a mail-order-bride ad with little luck. And after what happened with Miss Tender, I had the ad canceled right away. I may pursue it in the future if I don't have any other sort of prospects here in town," Dan said, giving Phoebe a lingering look before refocusing back on her brother. "It seems like a reasonable enough approach when Mr. Jenkins and Mr. Benning were both successful this way."

"I cannot deny that since both men have become happy husbands and fathers," Edward admitted with a smile on his lips. He enjoyed Mathew's company because they seemed to see eye-to-eye on many things. That and his son Mikey was always a joy to be around. And after Bailey had struck up a friendship with Brown Bear's wolf cub, things had been rather entertaining at the camp.

"Edward, may I have a moment alone with Mr. Mavis?" Phoebe asked as she looked up at her brother. They would be teaching together again in the morning and she felt like she wanted to say a few things to Dan before then.

"I'll meet you two inside," Edward said as he dropped Phoebe's hand from his arm. "I'll try to save us some seats."

"Thank you," Dan said as Edward nodded and stepped around them to join the throng still moving into the townhall.

"Dan, I wanted to apologize for the cold way I treated you yesterday and Friday. I was so confused by Miss Tender's actions that I really did think poorly of you afterwards even though I knew in my heart that you couldn't possibly be two-timing me," Phoebe said in a soft voice, causing Dan to step closer to her so he could hear her better. He always liked being close to Phoebe and was glad the time had finally come that he could speak privately with her.

"I appreciate your apology, Phoebe. It was such a surprising situation that I honestly don't blame you for thinking the way you did."

"But you have to understand why I was so quick to think that way. When I lived in Boston, I had been engaged to a man who I thought I truly loved and who loved me in return," Phoebe explained. Dan's breath stopped short in his lungs at the idea of Phoebe being engaged to another man. "I wanted to surprise him one afternoon for lunch, so I went to his home. There, I walked in on him being intimate with another woman in his sitting room."

Anger unlike anything Dan had ever known weaved its way through his body at the idea of Phoebe being treated in such a way. He saw the tears in her eyes as she spoke, and he knew it was hard for her to speak about such things. He clenched his fists and ground his teeth together, trying his best to get his anger under control. His mind told him there wasn't anything he could do right now about the situation, but if this man ever appeared in

Bear Creek, he wouldn't hesitate in beating him to a bloody pulp.

"That must have been truly difficult for you to bear," Dan said as he took Phoebe's hand in his, wanting to comfort her in some way.

"It only seemed to get worse from there because my father still insisted we marry to keep up appearances. Gavin didn't want a ruined reputation, and my father explained that wealthy men often took mistresses in order to deal with the stress of work. I was so appalled by both of them that I wrote to Edward, begging him to rescue me from such a life. And being eighteen, I was able to leave Boston the moment Edward arrived."

Dan stood there listening to Phoebe, rubbing his thumb over her knuckles while her hand trembled in his. He couldn't begin to imagine everything that Phoebe had been through, and now he thoroughly understood why Phoebe had become radically upset upon seeing him with another woman who was convinced they'd marry. If he had any idea about Phoebe's past, he would have gone to her sooner than this moment to explain the situation.

"I really don't know why I'm telling you all of this," Phoebe mumbled as she withdrew her handkerchief and blotted her eyes.

"Regardless, I'm glad you trust me with such burdensome details about your past," Dan said as he used his free hand to lift her chin up towards him so he could look directly into her honey colored eyes. "It helps me understand you a whole lot better. And I can honestly say I'm proud of the woman you've become here in Bear Creek. You didn't let your past destroy you and instead you've become a very respectable young woman." When Phoebe smiled brightly up at him, Dan thought that all the heartache for the last two days had been worth it because he'd finally discovered what had happened to Phoebe in Boston. And she'd been willing to tell him the details herself.

"Well, we better get inside before we miss anything or my brother comes looking for us," Phoebe said as Dan dropped his hand from her chin and eventually let go of her hand. He offered her his arm and she accepted as she placed her hand around his elbow to rest it upon his arm. Dan took a deep breath and let it out slowly, thinking he felt relieved to be on good terms with Phoebe once more.

"How about tomorrow after the children's lessons I ride with you back to the Indian camp? I could use some more Sioux lessons and I was wondering if you could tell me how the Indian children are actually doing with their own learning lessons."

"I'd be happy to help you in that endeavor. But you must promise to stay for dinner," Phoebe insisted.

"Then it's a date," Dan replied. They smiled at one another as they finally made it up the stairs of the town hall. They took a moment to speak to Pastor Munster, greeting him and catching up on the last few weeks.

"I pray for your students every day, Mr. Mavis. Bear Creek is surely lucky to have you as a schoolteacher. And I hear you're also teaching the Indian children English?" Pastor Munster asked.

"That's correct. And Miss James has been assisting me since she's familiar with the Sioux Indians and can speak their language," Dan explained, proud to have Phoebe by his side.

"Well, what a miracle. I see the Lord's hand in your two lives. You keep teaching those children, regardless of race, and God will bless you for your efforts," Pastor Munster said in a way to encourage the young people. He considered the Indians to be a part of God's people and liked to hear good stories of when the white settlers were finding ways to work with the Indians instead of oppressing them.

Dan then led Phoebe up the aisle to where her brother was

sitting in a front pew. When he'd woken up that morning, he wouldn't have thought he would be sitting in church with Phoebe and her brother. But after their special moment together, he was really glad he'd worn his best outfit to church in hopes of impressing both Phoebe and her brother. After all, if he was going to ask Phoebe to marry him one day, he'd need Edward's permission first.

THE NEXT DAY'S lessons passed by with relative ease, now that things seemed to be settled between Phoebe and Dan. She had actually been looking forward to returning to the town hall with the Indian children for the day's lessons. After the sermon yesterday, she and Edward had accompanied Dan to the inn for a lunch, which Phoebe had thought was rather nice of Dan to treat them both to a meal. Afterwards, it only left Phoebe with more excitement to spend time with Dan. She was starting to really think that he could be the one.

"Why do you keep looking at Mr. Mavis like that?" Squirrel asked her in Sioux, whispering softly to get her teacher's attention back to her since she'd asked Phoebe the same question twice.

Phoebe quickly turned towards the young girl, seeing the big smile on her face and knowing she'd been caught daydreaming about Dan while watching the man a little too closely. Phoebe felt like a foolish schoolgirl as her cheeks turned pink with embarrassment.

"I don't think I'm looking at Mr. Mavis any particular way," Phoebe replied in a soft voice. "Now, what was your question again?" Phoebe did her best to then focus on the lessons at hand and to help each child understand what Dan was teaching them.

She couldn't help but think that they made a good pair in the classroom and could really teach the children more effectively together. Mr. Franklin from time to time would take a break from his work in his office to see how everyone was doing. The children always enjoyed getting to talk with the Mayor, and the Indian children particularly liked to practice their English with him.

"Seems like things are settled between you and Phoebe," Mr. Franklin said in passing to Dan as he made his way back towards his office. Dan simply nodded as the Mayor went on his way. He looked at Phoebe then, being filled with so much relief that they were on good terms. He caught her gaze and smiled at her before returning to the lessons. He was eager to join Phoebe that afternoon and evening at the Indian camp and hoped he could learn from her how the Indian children were actually doing with their lessons and if he could do anything to help them learn more easily.

"Alright, students. That seems to be enough work for today. Make sure to write your assigned sentences tonight five times on your tablets and bring them in tomorrow for me to review," Dan said as he addressed the class. "You may all be dismissed now. Careful returning home."

The students talked excitedly together as they gathered their things to take home. Grasshopper was doing a swell job at speaking with his new friends who were sons of a farmer outside of town. It truly filled Dan's heart with pride to see the two races speaking with one another. Grasshopper had to ask his new friends to repeat themselves often, but the boys didn't ever tease Grasshopper or the other Indian children when they said something wrong or didn't understand them. He felt like everyone was really getting along now.

"Are you ready to head to camp?" Phoebe asked as she came

up to his desk where he was making a stack of all his notes and lessons plans before placing them in his messenger bag.

"I sure am," Dan replied as he finished collecting all of his things. He walked with Phoebe through the town hall and were then quickly approached by the Indian children who had just run back inside and were talking quickly in Sioux. As Phoebe listened to them, she hurried after them as they dashed out the front doors of the town hall to see that her horse and their Indian ponies had been cut free from their hitching posts and most likely scattered.

"This is dreadful," Phoebe exclaimed as she looked at the spot her horse had stood not that long ago when she'd first reached town. "Who would do such a thing?" She turned and faced Dan as he came out of the town hall after her, looking as confused as she felt.

"That's a rotten thing to do," Dan said as he looked at the children. "It seems we'll have to walk all the way to camp."

"But that will take forever," Phoebe said as she looked at the hurt faces of the children. "The horses are trained to return home, but it will be an awfully long walk for us."

"Let me go get my horse from the livery stables and I'll be right back. The children can take turns riding my horse and we'll try to think of a game to play with them while we travel back," Dan suggested.

"I'm willing to try anything," Phoebe called after him as he'd already started across town to fetch his horse. Phoebe turned her attention back on the children as she explained what probably had happened.

"There are people who still don't like us?" Grasshopper asked in his small voice. It pained Phoebe to admit such a thing to these children because they were still so young to understand the prejudice of white settlers.

"I am sure that there are many people who don't have good opinions about Indians. But regardless of those opinions, I think they try to still be good people. It is only a very small few who would do such a thing as to scatter our horses and make us walk all the way back to camp," Phoebe explained.

"But Mr. Mavis will be coming with us, right?" Squirrel asked.

"Yes, he will accompany us."

"Good. Because I'm worried about the people who scattered our horses. What if they are going to plan an ambush now that they know we must walk home?" she asked. Phoebe forgot that the children had all been trained to be good hunters. It's a part of their upbringing in their culture and it forced Phoebe to remember that these children were more than they appeared.

"I don't think these men would be so foolish as to try to harm us. Perhaps they'll try to make our lives miserable, but they won't harm us," Phoebe said, trying to reassure the children as they all looked at her with worried expressions on their faces. Just then, Dan came trotting back with his horse and quickly dismounted as he neared them.

"Alright, who would like to ride first?" he asked. A few of the younger children raised their hands, and Dan helped them up onto the back of his mare. The horse would easily be able to carry four children on her back, but that meant the other six children would have to walk the few miles to the Indian camp.

Together as a group, they set off towards the trail that led out of town and towards the camp. Dan asked the children to tell him the names of all the things they were passing in Sioux. He practiced saying the words and the children would all laugh when he became tongue tied. Then in turn, he'd practice speaking the words in English and the children would take their turns speaking the words back to him. Simple things like 'dandelion' and 'oak tree' became challenges for both him and the children, and though the walk was long, they passed the time laughing and learning new words.

Phoebe watched the interaction between the children and Dan, thinking that he would make a great father. The children were enjoying the game, and even though they had to walk uphill all the way to the camp, the children ran around collecting different things for Dan to try to speak in Sioux and that he had them speak in English. It was a rather humorous game that she enjoyed watching and it allowed her to really look at Dan without having to worry about him catching her. She was enjoying the experience just as much as he was.

The sound of horse hooves rattling against the ground further along the trail caused Phoebe to look up to see who was coming down the mountain. She saw several Indian braves quickly coming towards them and wondered what had happened to cause such alarm. She saw Brown Bear amongst the group and hurried up to meet them. They all came to a stop when they saw Phoebe and Dan walking with the children.

"Brown Bear, what is going on?" Phoebe asked as she spoke in Sioux, gesturing to the group of Indian braves.

"The Indian ponies that the children use to go to town came back to camp alone. We set out right away to find the children, fearing the worst," Brown Bear explained.

"Someone let all the horses loose outside the town hall. My own mare is missing," Phoebe explained. Speaking in English, she said, "Dan was kind enough to walk with us to the camp and even lent his own horse for the smaller children."

"Thank you, Dan Mavis," Brown Bear said as he focused on the schoolteacher. "I hope your horse had a good sense to make its way home as well."

"I'm confident I'll find her before too long. I'm surprised she didn't return with the Indian ponies," Phoebe said.

"Well, let the children ride with us back to the camp. I'm sure you and Dan could ride double on his mare," Brown Bear said with a twinkle of mischief in his eyes. Phoebe looked to Dan and he readily nodded. Together they helped the children off of Dan's mare and the Indian braves easily lifted them onto the back of their ponies. Then, Dan helped Phoebe up onto the saddle on his mare before mounting the horse behind her.

"I'm not used to riding without my side saddle," Phoebe said as she looked down at her feet and hoped that not too much of her ankles and legs would be showing as she rode astride the horse with Dan right behind her. He reached around her and took the reins and then flicked them to have the mare start after the Indian ponies.

"We should be pretty close to the camp about now," Dan reasoned. But he couldn't deny that he was enjoying being this close to Phoebe. His arms rested on either side of her as she held onto the saddle horn. Dan knew that if he looked down, he'd be able to see her exposed legs, but being a true gentleman, he didn't even risk peeking so that Phoebe didn't feel uncomfortable. With her back resting against his chest, Dan was doing his best to keep breathing easily. He thought this close proximity was very alluring and he imagined he'd enjoy an entire day riding out into the countryside with just him and Phoebe using one horse.

Phoebe did her best to focus on the trail in front of them as they followed closely after the small group of Indians. She was very aware of Dan right behind her and his strong legs pressed up against hers. It had been a long time since she'd been this close to a man and it reminded Phoebe of what more she still had to tell Dan about her past. She tried her best to keep her eyes focused on what was in front of her, but she couldn't completely ignore the heat she felt from Dan's body since they were so close together. Phoebe could reasonably imagine relaxing into his body and spending much time in a position like this.

The moment they reached camp, Dan slid off the back of the horse and helped Phoebe down. He hoped his cheeks were not as red as he thought they might be as he gripped his hands onto her waist to help her down. He wasn't sure why he was feeling so shy, but he walked silently next to Phoebe as they made their way through camp to let his mare loose into the corral with the other ponies.

As they then moved towards the central fire pit, Dan caught sight of Edward standing off on the edge of the camp, talking with an Indian maiden as he smiled down at her. The two of them looked rather familiar with one another, and when Edward leaned down and said something into her ear, he was starting to think that Edward had strong feelings for the other woman.

When Dan sat down beside Phoebe around the central fire, he pointed towards Edward and asked, "Is your brother courting an Indian woman?"

Phoebe followed his line of sight and saw Edward standing rather close to Morning Sun. She saw them and hoped that her brother was making some sort of progress with the Indian maiden when it came to their plans for the future together.

"Yes, that is Morning Sun. My brother has strong feelings for the woman and is trying to figure out the best way to move forward with her. In traditional Indian culture, the man who wants to marry a woman must present her father with a dowry of sorts. Usually it is either ponies he's stolen from other tribes or very nice hunting bows and arrows. But since Edward doesn't have any of those things, he's been trying to think creatively on what he's going to do."

"And what happens when Edward and Morning Sun do marry? Will they live here at the camp or in the place you're currently living?" Dan asked. He was starting to think that whatever Edward decided to do would greatly impact Phoebe as well.

"That is one more piece to the puzzle. The cabin we currently have is rather small, just big enough for the two of us. I wouldn't want to interrupt their private moments. However, if they do decide to live here at the camp, which is the most reasonable solution since it's all that Morning Sun knows and Edward doesn't mind being here, that means I'll either have to choose to live alone or move to camp as well."

"And what would you choose if that did happen?" Dan asked, not liking the idea of Phoebe living all by herself.

"I would choose to remain at the cabin. I love spending time here at camp, but I can't live the way they do. I very much prefer four walls around me at night instead of a teepee," Phoebe admitted. "Though it would be best for me to live at camp because it is the safest option."

"And I would readily agree with that line of thinking. Staying with the Indians might not be ideal, but it would only be temporary," Dan suggested.

"What do you mean?" Phoebe asked as she turned to look up at him.

"Well, certainly one day you'll marry, and you'll get to live in a home of your own."

"I wouldn't want to marry someone just because I preferred living in a house than a teepee or needed protection," Phoebe was quick to say.

"And I'm not saying that you should marry for those reasons. I simply wanted to state that your current situation is as temporary as you deem it to be."

Phoebe turned away from Dan, having not really thought

about marriage as a way to avoid having to rely on her brother. One of the many things she liked about Dan is that he was always so logical. He saw any problem from all sides and was quick to offer a solution. But since Dan was probably the only eligible man she'd consider marrying, she wondered if he was leading her down a very particular line of thinking.

"It's something to think about, is all," Dan added when silence fell between them.

Eventually Phoebe moved past the conversation and began teaching him different Sioux words. It was humorous when Brown Bear came near and Dan was able to practice a few words with the Indian chief, clearly surprising him. It took Brown Bear a moment to regain his awareness and he tried responding to Dan in the same manner and was pleased that Dan was able to understand him.

"The children will be pleased to learn that you are speaking Sioux now," Brown Bear said in English. "It shows them that it doesn't matter what age you are, you're never too old to learn something new."

"That was my intention, Brown Bear. I want to inspire and motivate the children to try their best each day," Dan replied.

"I think you are the perfect teacher for them, Dan Mavis. I only hope that there will be no more trouble in town concerning them." Brown Bear gave Dan a pointed look and Dan took it to heart. He'd speak with both the Mayor and Sheriff Benning tomorrow about the matter. After all, the Sheriff had made it clear to him that he wanted to know everything that was happening in town. Dan was certain the Sheriff would not be happy that he didn't tell him sooner about the horses being let loose and the children having to walk part of the way home.

As more people started to gather around the campfire for the evening meal, Dan continued putting his new Sioux knowledge to good use. Many found it funny and joined in on the entertainment, soon causing a small group of Indians of all ages to be sitting around Dan and Phoebe as they either listened to Dan speak Sioux or butcher a particular word pretty badly, causing everyone to laugh heartily.

"My word, I don't think I've had this much fun in ages," Phoebe said as she tried to control her mirth.

"It seems like you are not the only one," Dan replied as he continued to repeat the Sioux words that were spoken to him and Phoebe translated their meaning. They would laugh even harder when the Indians taught him dirty words and Dan and Phoebe would both blush deeply amidst their laughter.

"Seems like you're getting your boyfriend here in a lot of trouble," Edward said as he sat down next to Phoebe on the log. Morning Sun was close to follow and situated herself near him.

"Oh, don't you start, too. Dan and I are just friends," Phoebe said. But as she said the words, she felt as though they didn't fit right. Phoebe was sure that Dan cared much about her and she felt the same way for him. So, did that mean that they were now more than just friends? It would be something she'd need to ask him about later.

"Well, either way, it seems you're letting the Indians have their way with him," Edward said.

"It's all good fun," Dan said in their defense. "It's good to see everyone smiling and having a good time."

Eventually everyone had to get up to make room for the evening meal. Phoebe went to go help the women, along with Morning Sun, giving her time to speak freely with the woman that she was sure had captured her brother's heart. Meanwhile, the Jenkins' family made their way to camp and settled down next to Dan. Little Mikey toddled after Bailey as the dog sought after his friend while also keeping a close eye on Mikey around so many people and the large burning fire. But with so many people around, Mathew and Jenny felt comfortable allowing their son to move about the camp freely because all the Indians knew of the young boy and wouldn't hesitate in taking care of him.

"It's good to see you, Dan," Mathew said as he came to sit next to the schoolteacher. "I didn't know you'd be up here."

"I've been learning some Sioux words to try to inspire the children I am teaching to try their best at learning English. It's been a rather hilarious pursuit as the other Indian members have either been helping me or trying to teach me bad words," Dan said with a chuckle. Mathew nodded as though he could relate.

"When Brown Bear first started teaching me Sioux, he was a very diligent teacher. He was convinced that it was vital that I learned the language. But there are certain Indian braves who loved to teach me all manner of bad words and have me practice them with Brown Bear, thinking I was saying something nice when in reality I was insulting the man. Afterwards we all had a really good laugh, though."

"The Indians can be tricky like that, can't they?" Dan asked.

"They are very clever and mischievous to one another. It's how they keep each other on their toes, ready for whatever might be waiting to happen. It's all good fun in the end anyways."

They were soon joined by Margret and Mr. Fritz as well. It was surprising to Dan how many people from the town's community had shown up for dinner that evening at the camp. As he looked around, it appeared to him that none of the Indians seemed to mind. No one complained that they now had more mouths to feed. Everyone seemed to eagerly want to talk with one another and do their part in preparing the evening meal. Dan looked across the way and saw Phoebe working together with Morning Sun. She might not like the idea of living in the camp when her brother married, but she seemed to be at home amongst all the Indians.

"So, Mr. Mavis. What did I hear about you dressing like a slob Saturday morning and presenting yourself as such in town?" Mr. Fritz spoke up amongst their group. All eyes seemed to turn on him, and since he was already in high spirits, he figured it wouldn't hurt to explain himself. By the time he finished his story of why he'd dressed that way, there were many people who were laughing so hard that it took a while for them to catch their breaths.

"My word, who would have ever thought that a man would go to such lengths to get rid of a woman who clearly was excited about the idea of marrying," Margret said between gasps of air.

"You are very clever, Mr. Mavis. I will have to give you that," Mr. Fritz said after they were all settled once more.

When the meal was finished, Phoebe made her way back over to them, eager to catch up on what they had been discussing. Of course, that forced Dan to repeat his story once more and this time Phoebe was laughing so hard that she began to snort, which only spurred Dan on to laugh with her.

"I've never heard someone snort before," Dan said in a low voice, not wanting to embarrass her.

"Well, I don't do so very often, but it seems that it couldn't be avoided. No wonder Miss Tender went flying into the arms of another. You must have scared her quite a bit with your sudden transformation."

"I think it's the accent that really put her off," Dan said with another chuckle. Plates of food were then passed around and Dan was able to feast upon venison steak tips seasoned and cooked with various root vegetables. It was all covered with a type of corn gravy, and since the Indians didn't use conventional forks and knives, Dan was forced to use his fingers and carefully scoop up the food and eat it. He looked at Mr. Fritz and couldn't help but smile as the refined businessman really made a mess of himself. But Margret didn't seem to care as she passed him her handkerchief while laughing freely.

"I've never seen Margret laugh so much in my life," Mathew said as he leaned close to Dan. "Makes me think they are really getting along together."

"Certainly seems so. Do you think Margret would ever consider marrying at her age?"

"I think they might, actually. I know Margret enjoys staying with us on the ranch, but Mr. Fritz has a pretty large home close to town. She would probably enjoy being closer to her friends and having the privacy with Mr. Fritz if they do marry."

"Seems reasonable enough," Dan commented between bites of food. It seemed to him that there were plenty of couples around him that were getting along just fine with the people they cared about. He was glad he could be sitting there that evening with Phoebe by his side, but now that the situation with Miss Tender was all cleared up, did he really want to wait that long to tell Phoebe how he truly felt about her? As the sun was setting and the shadows were deepening around camp, Dan knew that he would have plenty of opportunity to speak with Phoebe and finally tell her how he felt about her.

When Edward stood and led Morning Sun away from the group, Dan figured that was his cue to try to get Phoebe alone. He passed his empty plate down the line of people to where the Indian maidens were gathering the dirty dishes to be washed. Phoebe stood to join them, but Dan reached up and stopped her, quickly standing with her as well.

"Phoebe, would you care to join me for a walk around camp?" he asked, trying to keep his nerves from bubbling up and stealing his voice.

"Yes, I'd like that very much," Phoebe said as she led him away from the central fire pit. "There is a trail that weaves around the perimeter of the camp. The Indian braves use it to keep an eye out for danger, but it's close enough to the camp that we shouldn't get lost in the setting sun."

"Sounds perfect to me," Dan said as he allowed Phoebe to take his hand in hers and led her a little way away from the camp. Once they stepped onto the nearby trail, Dan kept his fingers locked with hers as they walked, enjoying the feeling of the warmth of her fingers against his.

"I wanted to take the time to tell you something, Phoebe," Dan said as they walked at a leisurely pace. Phoebe looked up at him, squeezing his hand slightly to let him know that he had her full attention. "Ever since you first came to Bear Creek, I've had feelings for you. I thought you were absolutely gorgeous, but when you joined the book club, I was able to learn that you were highly intelligent as well. I would have asked you out on a date if every other man in town hadn't already. It was clear to me and the others that you weren't interested in marriage."

Phoebe's heart started to pound in her chest as she listened to Dan speak. It made her feel excited to know that Dan thought she was both beautiful and intelligent. And she had to agree with him that when she'd first arrived in Bear Creek that most of the single men in town asked her out one way or another, and she turned them all down politely with the explanation she wasn't interested in marriage. But to think this caused Dan to not approach her made her almost regret being harsh to the others.

"But after getting to spend these last few weeks with you teaching the children, I figured that it wouldn't hurt to try to express my own feelings for you. And after Miss Tender showed up out of nowhere due to my mail-order-bride ad, it really made me realize that I shouldn't have been pushing this off for so long.

Therefore, Phoebe James, I'd like to admit to you that I do care very much about you and hope you'll agree to us officially courting."

Dan stopped then and looked down at Phoebe, anxious to know what her reply would be. He felt like he was risking everything by expressing his desire to be with her, to hopefully one day marry her. If she denied him, he wasn't sure if he'd ever marry. He was certain he'd never meet another woman like Phoebe again. Or at least, he wouldn't here in Bear Creek.

"You're right, Dan. When I first came to Bear Creek, I was very against the idea of dating and getting married. I just couldn't trust any man that I dated because I'd just be reminded of Gavin and just be afraid all the time that I was going to be cheated on again. It was the first thing that came to mind when I saw Miss Tender for the first time. And though I do have very strong feelings for you as well and would like to officially court one another, I think there is something important you must know first about me."

Dan held his breath, his mind racing to anticipate what Phoebe was about to tell him. She'd just reciprocated his own feelings and he was eager to announce to the others back at camp that they'd started courting. But as he looked into Phoebe's eyes, he could tell she was hesitating to finally open up to him.

"It's okay," Dan said as he let out his breath. "You can trust me and trust that I won't tell anyone what you are sharing with me now." Phoebe nodded and tried to relax while forming the right words in her mind.

"One of the main reasons my father was highly intent on me marrying Gavin is because we had been intimate together. I'm not sure how he found out, but he did and told Gavin he had to marry me. Honestly, I thought it was a dream come true that I would be marrying the man I gave myself to. But, you know how the rest of that story goes. It seems that as soon as Gavin had what he wanted, he was done with me." Phoebe looked down at the ground, almost unable to see it clearly as the sunlight slipped away. She was glad that the rising darkness could hide most of her face and the shame she currently felt for not waiting until she was married to be with a man.

"I don't think you should ever regret what you did, Phoebe," Dan said, surprising Phoebe to where she looked up at him. At first, she thought he was crazy because she'd felt so much agony and heartache when realizing what Gavin had done to her and what her father was still willing to do. "If things hadn't gone the way they did, you wouldn't be here now with me, and instead you would have been stuck in a loveless marriage."

Just as a wide smile was spreading over Phoebe's face, Dan leaned down and captured her lips with his. She was so surprised by the sudden kiss, but allowed Dan to deepen his kiss as she wrapped her arms around his shoulders. Dan held her tight as he kissed her with every ounce of him, wanting to promise Phoebe the world and that he'd never treat her like the man of her past had. They were so lost in that kiss that they didn't hear someone approaching from behind them.

"I think that's quite enough, Mr. Mavis," came the dark voice of Edward James. Surprised, they both parted, though Dan kept his arm around Phoebe's waist. He wasn't at all embarrassed for the way he'd kissed her, wanting to convey his true feelings for her in that kiss.

"Phoebe has agreed to allow me to court her. It was the reason I decided to kiss her so," Dan explained, believing they were all adults and could speak freely.

"Is this true?" Edward asked his sister, completely in disbelief. He held a torch out towards them, shedding light into the space all around them.

"It is true, Edward. Dan did ask my permission and I did agree to it. I have told him about everything that happened in Boston and it didn't sway his intentions towards me," Phoebe said with a bright smile on her face. Edward studied her closely, trying to make sure she wasn't being pressured into doing anything she might regret later.

"I would have appreciated a little heads up, Mr. Mavis," Edward said as he looked back at the schoolteacher. Edward was very protective of his sister, but he had to admit he hadn't seen her this happy in a long time. And this was the first man she was considering after what happened in Boston. He figured that Phoebe would marry eventually, and if things went well with Dan, then perhaps that would make it easier for him to marry Morning Sun one day if he didn't have to worry about his sister any longer.

"Before I propose to Phoebe, if that does happen, I will make sure to come speak with you first," Dan promised. A thrill ran through Phoebe and she tucked her arm behind Dan as he did with her, thinking she would like that idea very much. But for now, they would continue to date with the intent of one day marrying if things went well. Phoebe had never been this excited about the idea of getting married, even back when she thought she was in love with Gavin.

"I'm going to hold you to that promise," Edward said with a nod. "Now let's get back to the camp before anyone else notices we've been gone for too long. Mrs. Phillips is a proper lady and she won't hesitate to send Mathew after you, Phoebe." She chuckled as she agreed, taking Dan's hand and pulling him after her as they all returned to the central firepit. There, Dan leaned towards Mathew once more and told him the good news.

"My goodness, it must be spring with all this love in the air,"

Mathew said with a chuckle. "Who would have guessed that soon it will be harvest season."

"Tell me about it," Dan agreed as he sat with Phoebe's hand in his, looking forward to the day when he could propose to her and finally have the wife he'd always wanted.

CHAPTER 12

The rest of the week seemed to pass by in a blur of happiness. Each day Dan rose early, excited about what the day would bring. He was getting very enthusiastic with his lessons, which the children all seemed to enjoy. And every minute that he got to spend with Phoebe seemed to be like a dream come true. Every morning he would place a kiss on her cheek, trying to avoid the children looking at them. But once, when he did quickly place a kiss upon her, he could hear all the children laughing widely and it took a good couple of minutes to get them all calmed back down again and focused on their lessons.

With each passing day, Dan thought more and more about how he'd like to propose to Phoebe. He hadn't thought of anything solid yet, and he was still planning on keeping his promise to Edward. As soon as Dan had a solid plan to propose to Phoebe, as well as a ring, he would first talk to Edward about his plan. It was something he thought about often, hoping he could think up the most perfect proposal for a wonderful woman such as Phoebe.

"I'm going to head over to Fry's for a few things while the children are out playing. Do you need anything?" Phoebe asked him one day as they had just let the children head outside for a break and to enjoy their lunch.

"Can you ask Mr. Fry if he has any mail for me? I haven't been there in a while and I've been thinking I better do that before I miss anything important," Dan said.

"Yes, I'll be sure to ask him for you," Phoebe said as she collected her handbag and headed out of the town hall. Phoebe felt like she was in the first real relationship of her life. She enjoyed spending time with Dan and could really picture herself being married to him. And this little errand to the general store made her feel like they were already married as she went to do something specific for him like get his mail. She was so beside herself with glee that she almost forgot that Standing Mountain was outside the town hall door and almost hit him with the door when she opened it.

"I'm so sorry, Standing Mountain," Phoebe said in Sioux. "I was daydreaming and forgot to let you know that I was coming out of the town hall."

"Is it a certain someone you are daydreaming about?" Standing Mountain teased in return. He was one of the few Indian braves that often came to town to trade with Mr. Fry. He was a familiar face around town and therefore had volunteered to stand watch over the town hall during the day so that no more harm could come to Phoebe's horse or the Indian ponies.

"I am not sharing those details with you," Phoebe replied. "I'm headed to the store. Do you want anything?"

"How about one of those peppermint candies?"

"Sure. I can do that for you." Phoebe chuckled as she crossed the road carefully and made her way up onto the porch of the general store. As she entered, she quickly said hello to Mr. Fry behind the counter and then found what she was looking for in a hurry. She didn't want to keep Dan waiting or alone with the kids just in case. Therefore, she set her purchases down on the counter and asked Mr. Fry for one peppermint stick as well.

"Someone has a sweet tooth today," Mr. Fry said with a chuckle.

"Actually, it's for someone else," Phoebe said. "Oh, and before I forget, Dan Mavis would like any mail he might have. I told him I'd bring him his letters if he had anything."

"Alright, let me look through the mailbox," Mr. Fry said as he bent down behind the counter and then slowly lifted the box he kept all the mail organized in that often came in a large bundle to Bear Creek. He then started thumbing through all the mail till he pulled up a small bundle for Mr. Mavis and then handed it to Phoebe.

"Wow, he certainly hasn't picked up any mail in a while," Phoebe said as she took the small bundle and her sack of goods.

"I would say he hasn't been in for about a week. Not ever since he came in and needed to send a telegram in a hurry."

"Well, thank you for all your help," Phoebe said as she collected her things and headed back towards the town hall. As she walked, curiosity got the best of her because she was hoping to get a sneak peek at the new books Dan had ordered for the book club. But as she started sifting through the letters, she realized that all the letters addressed to Dan were from different women throughout the East. Phoebe didn't know what to think of all the letters because she was certain that Dan had canceled his mail-order-bride ad. But there was certainly a lot of them and that made Phoebe rather upset.

"Here's your peppermint stick," Phoebe said as she

approached the town hall. She handed Standing Mountain the candy and then loaded her groceries into her saddle bags before heading back inside.

"Is there something wrong, Phoebe James?" Standing Mountain asked, seeing the distraught way she looked at the items in her hand.

"I'm not sure," Phoebe said before she went inside the town hall. As she crossed through the building, she could hear the children playing happily outside. Normally the sound would have been soothing to her, but all she could feel was a sense of dread rising up inside of her. Her palms were sweaty where she held onto the letters, and the closer she came to Dan and the children outside, the faster her thoughts were racing.

"Hey there," Dan called as she stepped out the back door. But when he saw how upset she looked, he left his spot on the grass where he was eating lunch and quickly came to her. "What's wrong?"

"You said you canceled the ad," Phoebe said softly as tears started to form in her eyes. She pressed the letters into Dan's hands as he looked down to see what she was talking about. He looked through all the letters, noticing the women's names and their addresses on the East coast.

"These must be leftovers from when I canceled the ad. It takes about two weeks for letters to reach this part of Montana and they usually come in piles," Dan explained. But as he saw a tear slip from Phoebe's eyes, he started to wonder what she was thinking in that moment.

"I don't believe you," Phoebe said as she took a step back from him. "I really thought I could trust you, but it seems you haven't given up on your pursuit to find your perfect wife."

"What? Come on, Phoebe. I just gave you a very logical reason why I received these letters. It's not like I'm going to open each one and respond to them. In fact, I've never responded to a single letter I've ever received from my ad." He took a step closer to her, but she only took another step back as her tears started to fall freely. Dan didn't think that she was thinking sensibly and was worried about what she was about to do.

"I can't do this anymore, Dan. I can't help you with the children only to come to these lessons and discover you're getting more letters from women. I can't go through all of this again when I try to trust a man and only get double-crossed in the end."

"Phoebe, you're letting your fears get the best of you. You need to see that this is nothing. Really and truly nothing. I placed an ad a long time ago and canceled it, and only received these letters because there is a gap in time when sending letters. But all of these are getting thrown in the trash and will be burned with the other papers that get used and are no longer needed." Dan was speaking softly, trying to calm the woman he truly felt for. "Here, take them. Go throw them away if you don't believe me."

"I don't believe you, Dan. And I should have never allowed myself to trust a man ever again," she said, her voice bitter. "I won't be coming to these lessons anymore, and I'm not agreeing to be courted any longer. By you or anyone else." Dan's temper was rising quickly as he went after Phoebe as she turned and went back into the town hall.

"You can't be serious, Phoebe. After all we've been through, all the tender moments together. You can't honestly compare me to that monster of a man you were once with. Don't make the mistake of throwing a perfectly good relationship away or letting your fears get the best of you," Dan called after her. Phoebe didn't stop or try to talk to him. He watched the stiffness in her shoulders as she quickly walked towards the front doors of the town hall.

"Fine! Have it your way! I couldn't marry a woman who

doesn't trust me anyways!" he then yelled, his anger and frustration finally getting the best of him. She finally stopped and turned to look at him, tears streaming down her face. It was such a look of grief and despair that he instantly felt bad for the things he'd said. They stared at each other for a moment longer before she turned her back on him and left the town hall in a hurry.

Dan was taking several deep breaths to try to get back in control of his emotions. He still had a yard full of students that would be coming back into the building for the rest of their lessons and he didn't want to cause a big scene. The last thing he wanted to do was have a repeat of what happened when Miss Tender showed up. Dan figured he could go on with the rest of the day and at least finish the students lessons. But when he went back out into the yard to see how the students were doing, even their happy faces couldn't help lift his spirits. He was truly feeling down and at a loss of what to do about Phoebe. She'd jumped to conclusions again and now he felt like there really wasn't a way they could come back from all of that.

After Dan was sure that all the children had taken the time to eat something, he called them back into the town hall to finish up their lessons for the day. They were talking excitedly when they came back in and filed into the pews, and Dan had to stare down at his notes in order to focus on his composure. He blinked his eyes a few times, doing his best to clear the tears that threatened to fall. He'd never felt like this and wondered if his heart was breaking for Phoebe. He wasn't sure if he'd be able to go on with the lessons but knew he had to do something in order to show the children that he was alright.

"Dillion," Dan said as he cleared his voice, addressing the oldest student in the room, "will you please read from chapter three in the book we are studying? Students, I want you all to follow along in your books and do your best to keep up with

Dillion. He'll make sure to read slowly." Dillion stood from his place in the pews and came to the front with his book in hand. After flipping through to the correct page, he waited for the other students to catch up, and then he began to read slowly so that the youngest of their group could follow along with the help from the others.

With that task at hand, Dan approached the Indian children and asked them to get all their writing tablets out. They started to practice the simple words they'd been learning in English, but at one point Grasshopper raised his little hand in the middle of Dan speaking, and too exhausted to scold the boy for interrupting, he simply asked what Grasshopper needed.

"Where Phoebe?" Grasshopper asked in simple English. Dan looked at the boy then, doing his best not to completely fall apart. He realized then that Phoebe had not only left him, but also left all the Indian children at the town hall.

"She went home," Dan said softly, having to look away from them for a moment as he rubbed his eyes as though they bothered him. Really, he was trying to do his best to keep from coming to tears.

"How we get home?" asked the oldest girl, Squirrel.

"I'll take you all home," Dan said as he pointed and gestured to all of them. Then he tried to say the same words in Sioux. It came out more like 'we go home' than anything. But the children all seemed to understand what he was trying to say. Dan realized then that Phoebe was a valuable tool in teaching the Indian children English. If she wasn't going to allow him to court her any more then perhaps she'd at least consider attending lessons so the Indian children had the highest chance at succeeding in learning English.

When the lessons were over for the day, the Indian children waited for him to gather his things and then go collect his horse from the stable before returning back to the town hall. Thankfully Dan was familiar with the trail by now and felt confident that he'd be able to get them all home safely. He just wasn't sure what he was going to tell Brown Bear when he reached the Indian camp.

"Is everything alright?" Standing Mountain asked when Dan returned with his horse. The Indian brave was one of the few Indians that could speak English besides Brown Bear.

"Yes. I told the children that I would lead them back to camp," Dan explained.

"What about Phoebe James?" Standing Mountain continued as he started to help the children onto their ponies.

"She went home," Dan said. He didn't want to say anything else until he spoke with the Indian chief.

"I can take the children back myself," Standing Mountain offered, thinking that something strange had happened and now Phoebe was clearly upset. She'd left the town hall in a hurry and hadn't even said anything to him as she mounted her horse and took off out of town.

"I need to speak with Brown Bear anyways," Dan explained. "I don't mind the ride to the camp."

"Then let us be off." Standing Mountain could tell that the schoolteacher wouldn't be willing to say anymore to him and he figured in time he'd learn for himself what had happened today. All together, they rode out of town, a feeling of foreboding settling over them all.

PHOEBE RODE HARD FROM TOWN, urging her horse up the mountain trail so she could get home as soon as possible. She could hardly believe what she was doing but couldn't deny the agony that was coursing through her body. She'd not only just left Dan behind, but also the Indian children. Guilt mixed with her emotions over discovering those letters for Dan. She felt so silly for not believing him, but even worse for the way she reacted. Phoebe was at such a loss for what to think was true or not that she hadn't even realized she'd made it back to the cabin till her horse was trotting into the stables as normal. Phoebe dismounted in a hurry and let the stable boy take care of her mare so she could flee inside.

The moment she was behind closed doors, Phoebe let the tears fall freely that she'd been fighting to keep at bay for so long. She stumbled towards the small dining table and slumped into a chair as she lay her head down on the cool surface of the wooden table. Her body shook with tremors from the emotional agony that was running through her. She hated the idea that Dan was writing other women when things had been so good between them. The idea of being his wife had grown on her so much that she was starting to become excited at the opportunity.

"How could I have done something like this?" Phoebe murmured to herself as she tried to get ahold of her raging emotions and the tears that seemed to be endless. She started to think about what Dan had actually said to her, that it was indeed logical that the letters were received simply because he'd canceled the ad sooner than the mail arrives in Bear Creek.

"But why did I get so angry that I wasn't willing to listen to him?" Phoebe said with a moan of pain at what she'd said to Dan. She knew now that what she'd done was very wrong, and even worse for leaving the Indian children behind like that. They would certainly want to know why she'd just up and left, and even though Standing Mountain was there to ensure the children's safety, it was still her responsibility to lead the Indian children to and from town. She'd not only let Dan down, but also the tribe, too.

When the front door opened, Phoebe looked up for a moment just to be sure that it was Edward and no one else. Brown Bear didn't really seem to knock anymore and just came right into their cabin. But as she quickly dried her eyes, she saw her brother standing in the doorway, covered in mining soot. His eyebrows were furrowed as he looked down at her, obviously concerned. And by the way she was crying, he had a gut wrenching feeling of who had caused her to be so.

"I'll kill him," Edward said as he closed the door behind him. "You just tell me what he did and I'll make him suffer for it." But his words only made Phoebe cry that much harder. He was eager to know why she was so upset and considered just leaving to seek the man out and beat the information out of him.

"I'm the one who did it," Phoebe managed to choke out amongst all her sobs.

"You? What do you mean?" Edward asked as he came closer to her. He didn't often like to track dirt into the house, but figured this was too big of an emergency to care about all the dirt he was covered in.

"I accused Dan of cheating on me again. He received more mail-order-bride letters today, even though he'd said he canceled the ad. He said they must just be leftovers and that he planned on throwing them away," Phoebe said as she gasped for air. Edward picked up his hat and tried to fan her face, afraid that Phoebe would faint from trying to speak and cry at the same time.

"I told him that I didn't believe him and I walked out of the town hall and left the Indian children behind. And he said that if I couldn't trust him that we couldn't get married anyways." Once Phoebe had finally finished explaining, she rested her head back down on the table to let her streams of tears continue to fall.

"Oh, Phoebe. That doesn't sound like something you'd do," Edward said in a calm voice as he started to rub her back with one hand and fanned her face with the other. "You just calm on down now while I go and get cleaned up. Then, we'll figure this out together." Phoebe didn't bother trying to respond. She just let all her pent-up grief and sorrow flow right out of her. She honestly didn't understand why she'd been so stupid. She should have never acted the way she did or spoke to Dan in such a manner. Plus, she'd turned her back on the children as well instead of at least staying for the rest of the lesson even if she was angry and upset. Now she was just frustrated with herself and her own stupidity.

"Alright now. I'm a presentable young man and ready to help you out," Edward said once he came back to the table in a fresh set of clothes and having washed all the soot from his skin. Phoebe leaned back in the chair, trying to straighten herself. But she'd cried so much that now her eyes were puffy and she had a strong headache forming quickly.

"Oh, Edward. I feel like a complete idiot for what I've done," Phoebe said as she used her handkerchief to dry her eyes and blow her nose.

"By the sounds of it, you jumped to conclusions and said some things you shouldn't have. Then, you didn't even bother listening to Dan when he tried to explain himself," Edward said, pretty much repeating everything that was swarming through her mind and making her feel like she'd made the biggest mistake of her life.

"I'm just so afraid of being hurt again that perhaps a part of me wanted to push Dan away before he got the chance to do it," Phoebe said, confessing to some of her darkest fears.

"Phoebe, no relationship is perfect. There will come a time when Dan is going to hurt you, but it won't be like what Gavin did to you. Dan's not the type of guy who would do such a thing, and I thought you knew that by now"

"I do know that, but I've been wrong before. What if I'm wrong about Dan like I was wrong about Gavin?"

"And what if you're not, Phoebe? What if Dan is the real deal, the type of man that all women dream about because he's loyal, faithful, honest, and sometimes even funny when he wants to be?" Edward smirked, remembering what it had been like to listen to him try to speak Sioux and the Indian braves teaching him words he shouldn't be saying. It had been a hilarious event that Dan had taken in good nature and hadn't been offended at all.

"I've made such a fool of myself. I love Dan but now I've really pushed him away because I've just been so darn scared of losing him, too." Phoebe's tears came back in full swing as she finally confessed her true feelings for Dan. She slumped forward and buried her face in her hands as a new wave of sobs went through her body. Edward moved his chair next to his sister and pulled her against him till she was clenching his shirt with her hands and crying into his chest.

When Edward had first shown up in Boston after receiving her letter, he had been ready to smash in skulls he was so angry. It was his anger that had driven him from the city to seek a way to tame his inner demons, having found a tribe of Indians that accepted him for who he was and were relatives to his deceased Indian mother. They had taught him to control his emotions, but entering his father's house and finding Phoebe in a similar state now had him almost losing full control and letting his anger run wild through him till he tore down every person who had ever hurt his dear sister. There wasn't a sweeter woman in all the world, and she deserved to be treated as such.

"Shhh," Edward said calmly to his sister, hoping she'd overcome her emotions and start to talk to him. He was willing to help her through this situation, like any other part of their lives together. But if she truly loved Dan and wanted to have a serious relationship with him, then she'd have to find a way to apologize to him and get over her past fears.

"What am I going to do, Edward?" she asked once her tears had finally run dry and she was too exhausted to cry anymore.

"You're going to have to first, finally, come to terms with what happened in Boston. It might have been years ago, but it obviously still affects you," Edward said.

"I've tried everything I can to forget those memories. But ever since I've started opening myself up to Dan, it seems like all of those horrible thoughts have come racing back into my mind," Phoebe explained. She slowly straightened herself as she rested against the back of her chair. She hadn't felt this horrible in a very long time and wondered if she'd ever be able to overcome this pain.

"Perhaps you need a spirit journey, something that White Raven would be able to help you with." Edward knew that the Sioux's medicine man was very talented and could surely help Phoebe where traditional medicine might fail her. Phoebe had once been given a bottle of laudanum to help her with her grief, but it had only made her very lethargic and no longer herself.

"What would that entail?"

"You'd have to ask White Raven. Sometimes it's a physical journey where you take a walk through the woods and come back when you've found your answers. Other times you're taken to a teepee to sit and meditate with a special cup of tea. But I found it very helpful for all the anger I used to hold inside of me. I might still be quick to anger, but it's not bottled up inside of me like it used to be."

Phoebe wasn't sure about Edward's idea, but if it would help her get over her past then perhaps she could have a real future with Dan. He was everything young girls dreamed of and she had been so stupid to suddenly push him away. She'd never been happier than she had been with Dan and spending time with him teaching the children all sorts of things. They'd laughed together and strived for the good of the Indian children. She felt safe with him and could even envision herself as his wife and he as her husband.

"And what happens after this journey? How do I make things right with Dan?" Phoebe asked after a while.

"Then you'll have to go to him with what you've learned on your journey. That's the whole point of it. To seek the answers you need but also gain the knowledge and wisdom to do what needs to be done," Edward explained, taking her hand in his. He didn't want Phoebe to ever be this upset again, especially when she had the same chance as him when it came to finding true love.

"Then I'll do it," Phoebe said with a sigh, squeezing Edward's hand before letting go. "Let's head to camp so I can talk to White Raven right away."

"Phoebe, you don't have to do this right away. Perhaps take a day or two to calm down your nerves first," Edward advised, rising with Phoebe.

"I've already wasted enough time grieving over Gavin and fearing ever being in another relationship. And now I've met a man I can actually fall in love with, who I know could love me truly in return. I've pushed him away and need to have him back in my life, Edward. I think enough time has already passed," Phoebe said, determined to make things right between her and Dan. But she also realized she wouldn't be able to move forward until she was able to let go of her fears of the past.

"If that's what you want, I'll go with you to camp. You might need a spirit guide anyways, and who better to guide you than your big brother," Edward said with a smile.

"Oh, I don't know. I'm sure White Raven will suggest the best," Phoebe teased back. After a moment, Phoebe embraced her brother, truly grateful for everything he'd done for her. Once again he'd come to her rescue and offered her a solution to her dire problems. She only hoped that he was right when it came to this spirit journey. She had answers she needed to find, and a relationship to mend at all costs.

CHAPTER 13

*D*an seemed to be walking through a haze the next few days. He would get up and get ready for his lessons, but his motivation and inspiration seemed to have drained from his body. He would make it to the town hall just in time to greet the students and get them started, but he wasn't there early enough to really get organized. His lesson plans were followed and constructed in a haphazard way, and after a few days, he feared he would never be the same without Phoebe.

The Indian children continued to come to and from camp with the help of Standing Mountain. He seemed pleased enough to ensure that the children still continued their lessons. And it was through him that Dan learned that Phoebe hadn't even been seen at camp since the day she left the town hall in a hurry. Sometimes it saddened Dan to think she was so hurt by her own grief that she'd put off all the things that she used to take pleasure from. And another part of him would get angry at her for giving up her responsibility to help teach the Indian children English. Thankfully, Dan knew enough Sioux words now that he could communicate with the children and continue to teach them. But it wasn't the same without Phoebe.

"Are you okay, Mr. Mavis?" asked Gravis one afternoon. Dan looked up from the book he had been reading out loud, but once he had become distracted from his thoughts, he'd started thinking internally instead of reading the book any longer.

He chuckled as he shut the book and shook his head. "It seems as though I'm a little preoccupied today. Would anyone else care to read?" he asked the class. A few students raised their hands eagerly and Dan allowed the children to take turns reading to one another and helping each other read. Even the Indian children joined in, which Dan thought was great progress for the class as a whole. But as Dan settled down in his chair and tried to focus on the book, he couldn't help but realize that his sulking was starting to affect major aspects of his day-to-day life. Would he ever see Phoebe again? Would they ever get a chance to talk about what had happened between them? Was it truly over?

Dan truly didn't know what to do. His heart still ached for Phoebe, at what they used to have. But his mind was still angry with her, that she still didn't trust him and had accused him of being something that he wasn't. He liked to think that he understood Phoebe, that she experienced something terrible by the hand of another man that was supposed to love her. In the end, her body and mind had been used for the pleasures of another. But how had he shown Phoebe that he was capable of doing the same thing? Didn't she know him as well as he knew her?

It was a relief when Friday afternoon came and Dan could dismiss the students for the weekend. Book club had officially been canceled till further notice because it finally reached his ears that members were no longer attending because they didn't agree with him that it was right to teach the Indian children English. When the Mayor had taken the time to explain to him what he'd overheard from Mr. Tibet, Dan had been crushed. It surely explained why all the regulars hadn't been coming, and since it was only him, Mrs. Phillips, Mr. Fritz, and Phoebe who had been attending, he'd posted on the town hall's bulletin board that the book club would be postponed until further notice.

Dan was gathering all of his things, his notebook full of lesson plans and his records he kept on every child and how they were progressing, when a very unexpected visitor came walking through the town hall doors. Dan had looked up from his desk when he heard the sound of the door opening, and when he saw Edward James enter, he'd assumed the man was coming by to meet with the Mayor. But when Edward continued on into the building and towards him, he wondered what Phoebe's brother had to say to him.

Dan finished putting his things in his satchel as he stood from his desk and slung the satchel over his shoulder. He would be ready to walk out if Edward had come to argue with him. But he seemed relaxed as he approached Dan and didn't seem angry at all. Dan wasn't sure what to expect, but he'd do his best to keep his composure no matter what.

"Good afternoon, Dan," Edward said as he came to stand in front of the desk, placing his hands in his jean pockets.

"Edward," Dan replied with a nod. "What can I do for you?"

"It's not what you can do for me, but what you can do for Phoebe." Dan raised one eyebrow at him, thinking there couldn't possibly be anything he could do for the woman. She hadn't shown up in town the last few days and for all he knew she had decided to remain at home in the mountains indefinitely.

"And what might that be?"

"We both know that Phoebe's past isn't a pretty one, and that her fears of what happened to her before might happen again. We can both see why she reacted the way she did, but I'm not here to defend her actions. I told her she was wrong and that she needed to get over her fears or you two won't have a chance in hell at a decent marriage."

"I can at least agree to that. I won't marry a woman who doesn't trust me, and I'm quite done being accused as someone I'm not," Dan replied.

"About the time my father finally told me that the woman who had raised me wasn't my mother, I already had a lot of anger issues. I was always getting in fights at school and never really seemed to have an outlet for my anger. And when my father told me how he slept with an Indian woman on a business trip just for fun, I really gave him a whopping of a lifetime.

"When he finally told me the tribe of my mother, I went in search of her. But by the time I located her tribe, she was already passed on. So, I spent time with her family and the medicine man of that tribe. He helped me go on a spirit journey that really helped me with my anger issues. I still get angry pretty easily, but it doesn't really affect me like it used to.

"Anyways, I told Phoebe that perhaps she should try it too to help her get over her fears of being cheated on again by the man she loves. These last few days she's been high in the mountain with White Raven and they won't be coming back down until she's finally overcome her fears."

Dan was surprised to hear all of this. He was learning more about Edward James than he ever thought he'd learn, even if he and Phoebe did marry. Dan never thought that Edward would open up to him like this. And what piqued his interest even more was the idea that Phoebe loved him. Was that why she was on this spirit journey? Was she trying to get over her fears so she could actually love him?

"So, what do you need me to do?" Dan asked, remembering the point of Edward coming to speak to him.

"Phoebe needs help on her journey. I tried to be there for her to be her spirit guide, but it's not working no matter how many times I try. And White Raven doesn't want to stop the process till she has succeeded. But after three days of no food and little to drink besides his special tea, I'm afraid she'll do more damage than good if they keep it up. This journey needs to come to an end, and I think you could be the one to help her finally overcome it all."

Dan was shocked at the severity of the situation. The thought that Phoebe was starving herself to go on this spirit journey didn't sound right to Dan. He understood that the Sioux Indians had a very traditional and cultural way of living that was a mystery to him, but this all sounded like madness.

"I'll help Phoebe if it means that whatever she's trying to do can be over. I don't understand what a spirit journey is, but I don't like the idea of Phoebe starving to death," Dan eventually said.

"Trust me, I feel the same way. That's why I came to you. I need you to come with me up into the mountains to be with Phoebe and help her finish this journey once and for all," Edward explained.

Dan gripped onto the leather strap of his satchel as he thought about all of this. He knew he didn't have any students to teach that evening and wouldn't be missing anything particular. But the idea of facing Phoebe again after everything she'd said to him and done, he wasn't sure if he was actually the ideal person to help Phoebe. However, he knew he couldn't turn his back on someone if they did truly need his help.

"Let me go collect my horse from the livery stables and I'll come with you," Dan said with a sigh. "I don't know how much help I can be, but at least I'll try."

"I knew you'd be willing to help out. You're the type of

person people can always rely on. That's why I already went and got your horse for you," Edward said with a chuckle. Dan simply smirked as he nodded, knowing that his willingness to serve others was also one of his biggest weaknesses.

Dan then followed Edward out of the town hall and sure enough saw his horse hitched to the post out front. After securing his satchel in one of the saddle bags, he pulled himself up onto the saddle and got comfortable before taking the reins and leading his horse after Edward.

"So, how far up on the mountain will we be going?" Dan asked as he looked towards the peak. He didn't know anyone who had climbed all the way to the top and he wasn't particularly fond of the idea of going up that high.

"First, we are going to the camp. You'll need to be cleansed before we can approach White Raven and Phoebe. You'll be given new clothing and then smudged with the smoke from sage and different herbs. Then, we'll hike up through the mountain pass to a ledge where Phoebe and White Raven are," Edward explained.

"This seems very ceremonial," Dan commented as he urged his horse forward to keep up with Edward's pace.

"It is in a way. An Indian man or woman usually only goes on one spirit journey in their life. Brown Bear says he's gone on four in order to be a great chief for his people. It is one of the reasons he feels like the Great Spirit talks to him so often because he's taken the time to travel to the Spirit World during these journeys and feels very connected to the other side."

"That's surely interesting," Dan admitted. He wasn't familiar with the Indian's religious beliefs, and he surely didn't see any of the Indians attending Pastor Munster's sermons. But if the pastor could see everyone as God's children, then Dan knew he could as well.

"When you say new clothing, does that mean I'll be dressing up as an Indian?" Dan asked after a while. Edward chuckled as he turned towards Dan in his saddle and nodded.

"You'd be surprised how comfortable the leggings and tunics are. I'm sure you're going to enjoy the experience."

"If you say so."

REALITY and the dream world blended so well together that Phoebe could no longer understand the concept of time or what was real and what wasn't. She hiked all the way up the mountain with White Raven after agreeing to undergo this spirit journey. The medicine man had seemed to be expecting her when she'd traveled to camp with Edward that evening which seemed so long ago. She'd been given traditional Indian woman's clothing to endure the journey and had stood still in her new clothes as the women cleansed her in the smoke of sage. It had been a slightly sweet smell, yet something so completely unusual that she couldn't put her finger on the scent.

Edward had led the way through the darkness with a torch in his hand. Phoebe had followed behind him and White Raven took up the rear as he carried a small pack on his back. He had explained that they would need very few things, but that they shouldn't wait till morning. Therefore, they had traveled towards the top of the mountain during the night, each step seeming to surround them in more darkness and the bitter cold of night.

When they'd reached the stop, White Raven was quick to gather enough wood to start a fire from Edward's torch. Then, he placed a small water pot on the fire and went to work brewing some sort of tea that smelled very strong and pungent. When White Raven poured three cups and handed them out to each person, Phoebe had been grateful for something warm in her hands. Yet, she wasn't looking forward to drinking the tea.

"Once you begin, you must not stop till you find the end. Your brother and I will be with you to guide your spirit through the spirit world so you can learn what you must to overcome your darkest fears," White Raven explained in Sioux. "Your body will remain, but your spirit will drift away to go on this journey. During that time, I'll continue to have you drink this tea, but you may not remember waking long enough to do so."

"How long do you think this will take?" Phoebe asked, a mix of dread and anxiety coursing through her. Did she really want to do this? But when she thought of Dan and how badly she'd probably hurt him, she knew that she had very little other choice.

"It can take a few minutes, hours, or even days. The concept of time will become irrelevant, but your body will remain safe," White Raven explained.

Eventually, Phoebe put her lips to the rim of the small clay teacup and forced herself to drink every last drop of the bitter tea. She wiped her mouth on the back of her hand when she was done, thinking it was rather unladylike. And with that thought came another, and another, till she was allowing her body to drift back onto the solid ground just long enough for her to close her eyes and let go of everything.

And now she was stuck in this place. At first it felt like she was dreaming, following a trail through the woods as the sun hung overhead. But no matter how far she traveled, the sun never moved, and she never seemed to get very far. Sometimes she'd see different animals moving up ahead and try to get near them to make out their appearance. But the closer she tried to come towards anything, the further away it seemed to appear. Sometimes she'd even go back and sit with White Raven to drink more tea, but he'd never speak to her and only sat and meditated before the fire pit. And no matter where she looked, she never found Edward.

The sound of running water caught her attention at some point. She hadn't heard water before and couldn't fathom how she'd missed it before. Having to step off the path through the woods, she pushed her way through the brush and threatening branches of oak trees. But eventually she made it to a clearing where there was a waterfall rushing water into a small pool below. And on the edge of that pool stood Dan in what appeared to be Indian clothing.

"What are you doing here?" Phoebe asked, the first words she'd spoken since she'd found herself in this place. Dan was the last person she would have expected to see and wondered if this was all a part of the dream she was having. Dan turned at the sound of her voice and he smiled at her, making Phoebe feel even more dreadful for what she'd done to him.

"I came to help you," Dan said as he took a couple of steps closer to her. "My word, you sure look beautiful in those clothes." Phoebe stopped a moment and looked down at her body, having forgotten she was dressed in an Indian woman's gown with leggings. They felt soft as she rubbed her fingers over the clothes.

"You don't look too bad yourself," Phoebe said as she looked back up at Dan. Even for a dream, she thought she could picture him perfectly before her. He was taller than her, but not by much since she was tall for a woman. Yet, it was nice to be around a man that was taller than her. His blue eyes bore into hers, making her feel almost see-through, as though he could read her mind if he tried to.

"I've missed you," Phoebe confessed as she closed the distance between them. "I've been here for so long, wondering around and around that it's so nice to finally be able to talk to someone."

"Have you found what you're looking for?" Dan asked as he extended a hand towards her. She took his hand in hers, wondering why she didn't feel any warmth at his touch.

"I don't know. I'm not even sure what I am looking for," Phoebe confessed.

"Is it me you're looking for?" came such a dark voice that Phoebe felt shivers run up and down her body. Her eyes went wide as her mind tried to fathom how he had found her.

Phoebe let go of Dan's hand and turned as she saw Gavin slowly approaching her from the thick brush. He was dressed in the same fine business suit he always wore. A lopsided grin was on his face, the one she'd fallen in love with. She used to enjoy those lips on her bare skin, but now the very sight of him made her want to vomit. As Phoebe glanced behind Gavin, she was sure she saw another figure hovering right outside the tree line, and that mystery figure made her even more nervous.

"How did you find me, Gavin?" Phoebe asked, wishing she could finally wake up from this dream. He was the last person she ever wanted to see again.

"Like it has ever been hard for me to find you," he replied with a chuckle. "I found you alone at Mr. Newton's ball that one spring day. Dear Lord, didn't we just have the best night ever."

"Stop that! You are a liar and a heathen. I want nothing to do with you ever again," Phoebe said as she took a step back from him. But as she looked over her shoulder, she saw that Dan was now no longer to be seen. She was afraid when she realized she was now alone with Gavin.

"Then why am I here, Phoebe? If you don't want me, then why am I here?" Phoebe stared at him, not understanding his question. After all, he was the one that had found her, not the other way around.

"What do you want, Gavin? The last time I heard anything about you, you'd married the woman you cheated on me with."

"You mean Annabelle?" Gavin asked as he gestured towards the woods. The woman Phoebe had glanced being intimate with Gavin then appeared, coming to Gavin's side and placing an arm around his waist. Gavin turned to her and lowered his lips to hers, kissing her with a passion that Phoebe never wanted to see ever again. She looked away, unable to watch them as the pain she'd first felt upon witnessing them together overcame her body and caused her much discomfort in her chest.

"Oh, come now, Phoebe. Is it really that hard to imagine that I'm with another woman now?" Gavin asked, pulling Phoebe's attention back to him. She looked around quickly and found that Annabelle was no longer around. It was a small relief, but she was still faced with Gavin.

"I don't care anymore, Gavin. That was years ago. I have a new life now and I never have to worry about you again," Phoebe said as she crossed her arms over her body.

"I can certainly see that," Gavin said as his eyes roamed over her body. There was a time when she had loved when he did that to her, but now it only made her skin crawl and itch. "Who would have thought that Miss Phoebe James would ever be caught dead dressed as an Indian? And worse, to hear that you speak their language and associate with them."

"Like I care what people think? I'll never be going back to Boston, so it won't matter what society deems of me. Here I'm free to be whatever I choose to be."

"And what have you chosen to become? A coward? A fearful woman who is unable to love again? Seems like you've found yourself in a world of trouble." Phoebe felt shocked to hear

Gavin say these things. Half of her mind wanted to know who had dared to share this information with the man she now loathed more than anyone in the world. And the other half of her mind was scrambling to find a good explanation for herself. She had to keep reminding herself that this was all a dream, that this wasn't real. But the fear pounding in her heart felt very real.

"I am not those things, Gavin. After all, I stood up to you and my father when the man was still going to force me to marry a man like you," Phoebe said, trying to gather up all her strength and courage.

"And would that have been really all that bad? You'd be living in the luxury you always knew, I'm sure I would have still been affectionate with you from time to time. You would bear all my children and find a sense of happiness with them that you'd no doubt not find in me. After all, I have particular itches that need to be scratched by other beautiful women." When he laughed, Phoebe got the urge to beat him with her own two hands. But the thought of touching him caused her to stay rooted in her place next to the pond of water, the water falling down seeming to be like a distant sound.

"I'm happier here than I ever was in Boston," Phoebe eventually said.

"But that brings us back around to the original question. Why am I here? If you were so happy, why did you push Dan away?"

Phoebe could feel the tears pushing themselves up to the surface once more and the last thing she wanted to do was ever be found crying by Gavin again. She knew he wouldn't take pity on her, and so she did her best to push those tears away.

"I was afraid that Dan would turn out to be just like you," she finally confessed. "I'm terrified of one day coming home to find him with another woman."

Gavin shrugged his shoulders, seeming to really not care

about how she felt. "You're afraid you'll marry a man just like me, and yet not find out about his nasty habits till things are already official."

"Yes," Phoebe gasped, feeling the agony of her fears boiling to the surface of her skin. "I'm so afraid of having my life ruined all because I decided to love once more."

"And surely your father was never a good example of what a husband should be. After all, you and Edward are half-siblings."

"And who knows how many more women he cheated on mother with?" Phoebe added. "He and you are the same."

"Yet, what about me and Dan?" Gavin asked. At the mention of his name, Dan seemed to reappear. This time, he came to stand next to Gavin, making Phoebe think that it was such an unpleasant sight. She was being faced with both men she ever loved. She knew that Gavin was a vile person, and as she looked at Dan, she thought how wonderful he was. He had been the perfect gentleman, even taking the time to ask for her permission before kissing her on her hand for the first time. He had always been kind and considerate to her that, standing before them both, how did she ever think that Dan could ever be like Gavin.

"You two are nothing alike," Phoebe said in a stern voice, letting her fear wash off of her skin. It was calming and soothing to say those words out loud and to let her fear finally go. "Dan has more kindness in his pinky finger than you have in your entire body."

"Kindness isn't everything," Gavin said with a shrug of his shoulders.

"Virtuous, considerate, charitable, knowledgeable, intelligent," Phoebe said as she took small steps forward, wanting to fight Gavin back with her words alone. "An overall decent human being that I've fallen madly in love with. And I let that love scare me to death and now I'm more afraid that I've lost

Dan forever instead of the idea that he could ever possibly hurt me like you have."

Phoebe was breathing hard when she finished speaking. Gavin looked at her, his hands tucked into the pockets of his trousers. He was so handsome that it wasn't hard to imagine how he found his way into the arms of many women. But as she looked at him, up close for the first time in years, all she felt in her body was this untamed rage towards him for causing so much damage in her life, even years later.

"See, was that really so hard to figure out?" Gavin said as he turned towards Dan. "She's all yours, cowboy." And like that, Gavin vanished from sight. She thought his exit was rude since Dan wasn't a cowboy, but a very skilled schoolteacher.

"A part of me wants to ask how you could have ever fallen for a man like that," Dan said as he gestured towards the area that Gavin had just occupied.

"And what does the other part of you want to ask?"

"Do you really love me?" Dan asked as he came towards her, lightly setting his hands on her hips as he drew her to him.

"Yes, Dan Mavis, I truly do love you," Phoebe replied, finally feeling free from all the fear she'd kept bottled up inside of her for years.

"Do you trust me, though? Do you trust me enough to never doubt my love and devotion to you, that I'll always be a loyal husband and a very doting father?" Dan asked in a very pleading voice, as though he was desperate to know for sure, once and for all, that Phoebe would never hurt him like this ever again.

"Yes. I know I can trust you with my life, and also my heart. You are nothing like Gavin or my father, and therefore I should never have to fear one day coming home to you being with another woman," Phoebe said, her words banishing her fears once and for all.

"Good. Because I would never do something like that to you, Phoebe. I'm going to love you openly for the rest of my life, and each day you shall know of my love for you and never be able to doubt that I'm the one you've been looking for all your life." As soon as Dan finished speaking, he lowered his lips to hers as she pushed herself up onto her tiptoes. She wrapped her arms around his shoulders and held him close as she kissed him freely, feeling a deep sense of love pass between them. She'd never felt anything like this before, even during the times when she'd allowed Dan to kiss her before. Now, she felt like nothing was holding her back as she freely gave herself to Dan.

CHAPTER 14

*a*s Phoebe finally opened her eyes, she felt her vision fighting for control as waves of dizziness washed over her. She tried to sit up and placed her hands firmly onto the ground to keep herself from tumbling over. She felt the flames of a fire nearby and didn't want to accidently fall into the fire.

"Careful now," came Edward's voice as his hands guided her into a seated position. He knelt next to her and allowed Phoebe to rest her head on his shoulder.

"I feel like I'm going to be sick," Phoebe said as she tried to focus her eyes on something so she'd stop feeling like she was spinning in circles.

"It will pass, I promise it won't last but a few more minutes," Edward said as he held onto her tightly.

"Drink this soup," White Raven said in Sioux as he came close to Phoebe and pressed a clay bowl into her hands. It felt warm and she was grateful to finally be feeling something in her hands again. Carefully, she raised the soup to her mouth and drank the broth as though she hadn't eaten in days. She felt very hungry all of a sudden and used her fingers without embarrassment as she ate the bits of meat and the root vegetables in a hurry.

"My goodness, why am I so hungry?" Phoebe asked as her vision seemed to steady. She was able to see clearly now and could peek over the ledge of the mountain and see that the sun was coming up. "Is it already morning?"

Edward chuckled as he looked at the rising sun, wondering the best way to explain things to Phoebe. "It is the fourth morning after we first came up to this spot. You've been dreaming ever since then and haven't had anything to eat. White Raven has been giving you sips of the tea in your mouth, but that is all."

"You have to be kidding," Phoebe said as she looked up into Edward's eyes, wondering if he was playing some kind of joke on her. But as her bladder protested, she wondered if there were some truth to his explanation.

"Here, have another bowl," White Raven said in Sioux as he took Phoebe's empty bowl and pushed another into her hands. Once again, Phoebe ate the entire contents with gusto, making White Raven chuckle.

"Have I really been asleep for three days?" she asked White Raven. The older medicine man simply nodded as he went to go refill the bowl. He then moved to the other side of the fire and pushed the bowl into Dan's hands. She hadn't noticed that he was there before, and when she noticed what he was wearing, she was completely shocked.

"Why are you dressed like an Indian?" Phoebe asked, addressing Dan between bites of food.

"Because your brother told me it was all part of what I needed to do to help you through your journey," Dan replied in a soft tone. He looked exhausted, and she was sure that she didn't look much better after laying around for three days.

"I had the strangest dream that you were wearing Indian clothing, and now here you are just like in my dream," Phoebe said as she finished the food, starting to feel more like herself.

"You mean the dream where you finally confessed that you love me and are no longer afraid of loving me?" Dan asked with a smile. Phoebe's mouth fell open as she stared at Dan as he carefully ate the soup. Their eyes locked and Phoebe tried hard to fathom what he was saying.

"How were we able to share the same dream?" Phoebe asked White Raven in Sioux. The medicine man chuckled again, liking how surprised the white settler was.

"Because your souls are joined together and have been from the beginning of time. It was only Dan who was able to journey with you, to sleep and dream with you in the Spirit World as I guided your two souls together. Not even your brother was able to do that," White Raven explained.

"But it's impossible," Phoebe said, trying to think logically.

"Really? Then why did it happen?" White Raven asked with a grand smile on his lips. He was thoroughly enjoying this reaction.

"What else did you see?" Phoebe asked as she turned her focus back on Dan.

"I saw a lot, Phoebe. But we don't need to discuss that right now," Dan admitted, not wanting to startle Phoebe or make her feel uncomfortable.

"Did you see him?" Phoebe asked, wondering just how much Dan had seen of her dream. Dan nodded as he ate, also feeling rather hungry all of a sudden. Though he hadn't been asleep as long as Phoebe had.

"How are you feeling?" Edward asked, drawing Phoebe's attention to him.

"I'm fine, I guess."

"But what about your fear? Do you think the spirit journey actually worked?"

"I think it did," Phoebe said as she looked at Dan. Before she would have felt such fear to confess her feelings for him. But now she felt as though a weight had been lifted off her heart and she could love without ever fearing her past again.

"Then this has all been worth it," Edward said with a sigh. He pushed himself to his feet and stretched, looking as exhausted as she felt. "I'm going to head down the mountain and meet with the miners. I'm sure they're all wondering where I've been for the last few days."

"Thank you, Edward, for risking so much for me," Phoebe said as she raised her hand and took his hand in hers, squeezing it for a moment before letting it go again.

"It's always been worth it to see you happy, Phoebe. And I know you'll be much happier now that everything has been cleared away from your past," Edward said in a comforting tone. Phoebe watched as Edward nodded towards Dan before making his way down the trail that would lead back towards camp.

"If he is leaving, then it seems I can go as well," White Raven said in Sioux. "I will leave these things for you, but you must promise to return them to me when you come back to camp."

"Yes, White Raven. I promise to return your things. Thank you so much for everything you've done for me and Dan," Phoebe said with a kind smile.

"It's always my pleasure to help a beautiful young lady," he said with a chuckle. Then, White Raven stood and took a few things with him before following after Edward. She would always be thankful for that medicine man and what he'd been able to do for her. She might never come to understand it, but she was certain that he'd done something absolutely miraculous.

"Do you think we should get going, too?" Dan asked as he slowly made his way over to her to sit beside her near the warm fire. The morning was still cold and having slept on the cold ground all night made his body very sore.

"I don't know about you, but I don't even know if I can stand up yet," Phoebe said as she moved her legs from side to side, feeling how weak they were.

"Well, I'm not in a hurry right now. I don't have any tutoring to do today so I think it would be nice to just sit here for a while," Dan said as he looked towards the rising sun, thinking he'd never seen a nicer sunrise. He wasn't pleased with the height in which they currently sat, but he tried not to let himself grow uneasy from it.

"That's good news. It's going to take me a while to get up and moving again," Phoebe said as she moved a bit closer to Dan. Then, she laid her head down on his shoulder, wanting to be near him. Dan took the open invitation and wrapped an arm around Phoebe, feeling the soft Indian gown that she wore and thinking it was a nice feeling.

"So, you love me?" Dan asked after a while in a soft voice.

"You know I do. You were there, after all," Phoebe replied.

"Yes, but I still wanted to hear you say it in reality." Phoebe lifted her head from his shoulder then and looked up at Dan, making sure to look directly into his beautiful blue eyes.

"Dan Mavis, I love you," she said softly.

"And I love you, Phoebe James," Dan replied before placing a kiss to her lips. It wasn't hungry or needy, just a pleasurable kiss upon her lips. She reasoned she could have sat there all day just feeling his kiss upon her lips, but the sudden call of nature raged through Phoebe till she couldn't ignore it any longer and had to break the kiss.

"I'm going to go take care of my needs," Phoebe said with a sheepish smile on her lips. "I just need help standing up."

"Oh, certainly," Dan said as he stood and then slowly helped Phoebe to her feet. Her legs felt wobbly, but as she stood for a second and simply held onto Dan, her strength eventually returned. And once she was steady enough, she started to walk away from the fire till she could find a decent spot to take care of herself.

While Phoebe was gone, Dan sat by the fire and helped himself to another bowl of soup. He'd never done anything like this before, from cooking a meal on top of a mountain to wearing Indian clothing. It all seemed rather strange, but he was glad he could experience it with Phoebe.

"Hey, you need to come see this," Phoebe said when she returned to the campfire. Her hair hung in ringlets down her shoulders and back. Her womanly figure was easily seen through the fitting Indian garments, and though he'd seen her dressed finely in a silk gown, Dan thought she'd never looked more beautiful than how she looked right now.

"You know, I think the Indian clothing suits you," Dan said as he stood and came towards her. He reached out his hand and let his fingers glide through her hair. "You are truly a beautiful creature."

"Thank you," Phoebe replied as a deep blush settled over her cheeks, making her even more alluring to Dan. "Now, come on," she said as she reached up and took his hand and led him through the forest. The sound of running water could be heard and for a second Dan thought that the sound was a bit familiar.

As Phoebe led the way and passed through into a clearing, a surprising sight then was before Dan. It was the same clearing that he'd seen in Phoebe's dream, of a waterfall cascading down into a shallow pool. From there, the water ran off down into a small creek.

"I wonder if this is how Bear Creek got its name?" Dan said as he approached the water. "Perhaps this is where the creek starts?"

"I simply think it's odd that I dreamed of this place and now it's here all of a sudden," Phoebe said as she let go of his hand and neared the water's edge. She kneeled before the water and cupped her hands together to form a cup so she could drink from the clear water. Dan joined her and did the same, thinking that it was perfectly cold and refreshing.

When Phoebe stood back up and turned around, she could see the spot where Gavin once stood. Being in this place made her dream that much more real to her and she wondered just what exactly she had experienced. She shivered, thinking she'd faced Gavin again. Phoebe was certain she didn't want to go on another spirit journey and would be satisfied with just one. He'd been so real in her dream that she wasn't sure if she could handle another encounter and still be as brave as she had felt in that dream.

"Do you think you're ready to head down to the camp now?" Dan asked as he came to stand behind Phoebe, this time wrapping his arms around her waist and holding her to his chest. She placed her hands on his, relaxing into his body as she looked around the clearing and the tall trees that seemed to hide this place from sight.

"Yes, I think it's time. It might be slow going, but I don't think either one of us is in a rush," Phoebe said.

"You're right. We'll take our time," Dan replied.

After one more look around the clearing, at the magnificent waterfall and the pool of water underneath, Phoebe walked with

Dan back to the small firepit and started to get ready to go. They took the time to eat the rest of the soup and clean all the bowls and pots in the pool of water. Once everything was clean and ready to go, they packed it all up in the small pack White Raven left for them and made sure that the fire was completely out. It would be devastating if a forest fire started at the top of the mountain, consuming everything below.

Once ready, together they took the trail leading down the mountain that would take them back to camp. Despite wearing moccasins on her feet, Phoebe thought she was able to walk with ease since the path was well worn. It made her wonder how many people came to the top of the mountain for spirit journeys or simply to go to the waterfall. Phoebe thought she'd like to return in the summer when the days were unbearably hot. It would be nice to go swimming up there and enjoy the cool water.

"I think the Indian children will be excited to see you," Dan spoke as they walked together. He had been taking in the scenery around them now that it was daylight and he could see things easier. He always found the forest on the mountain to be alluring and even relaxing as birds flew overhead, sending their bird song far and wide. The sound of water flowing could be heard from the small creek, and even though he was quite exhausted from the intense dreaming he'd experienced last night, he thought it was going to be an absolute splendid day now that he'd declared his love for Phoebe.

"I'm going to be excited to see them as well. I want to apologize to the students for leaving the way that I did earlier this week. They deserve an explanation," Phoebe replied.

"It might be hard for children to understand adult emotions. But I know you'll do your best," Dan said as he took Phoebe's hand and laced his fingers with hers. He'd been walking pretty slowly to allow Phoebe the opportunity to take her time. After all, she'd pretty much been in a coma for the last few days, and though the exercise was good for her, he didn't want her falling ill again from exhaustion.

"How have they been in school while I was dreaming?" Phoebe asked.

"Pretty good. Learning Sioux really helped me communicate with them so I could continue their lessons. But all the children seemed to sense that I wasn't really doing my best this week. They will be happy to see both of us back in the classroom next week, and in much better dispositions," Dan explained.

"And we need to get the book club back together. I don't care what anyone thinks of us teaching the Sioux children. Even if Mrs. Phillips and Mr. Fritz are the only two members, then I'm okay with that. They're good company anyways."

Dan was really liking the passion in Phoebe's voice. She sounded so much more optimistic and ready to get to work. It was as though her soul had been set free and now she could look forward to the future with a happy heart. There would come a time when Dan would need to talk to Phoebe about what he had seen and what it meant to her, but for now he understood the point of it all.

The moment they returned to the camp, a little tired from the long walk, they both seemed to be swarmed by the tribe. Everyone was eager to see them and to learn how Phoebe's spirit journey had gone. Dan was quick to realize how special this experience had been and how all the Sioux people were willing to help Phoebe out as she recovered. Someone took the pack from Dan and promised to return it to White Raven, especially when Phoebe protested that she needed to return it herself. They were both led over to the central fire where they were given plenty to eat and drink while the others chatted with them excitedly.

"What was it like, Phoebe James? Who did you see in your spirit journey?" one maiden had asked her in Sioux.

"It was like dreaming for a night. I had no idea I was up there for three days. But when it comes to what I saw, that is something I do not wish to speak about," Phoebe replied.

"Ah, I can't wait to go on a spirit journey of my own. The moment I have a worthy reason to go on a spirit journey, I shall go up the mountain with White Raven and see my whole life ahead of me," the maiden said excitedly as she helped fill Phoebe's plate with corn-mash and venison. There was a spiciness in the water that she was drinking, and when she asked what it was, the maiden explained that it had been soaked in the last berries of the year with honey and cinnamon bark. Phoebe thought it was lovely and savored the unique gift.

"It seems the schoolteacher has returned," came Brown Bear's voice as he came into the area around the central fire pit. Many of the maidens who had been sitting with Phoebe said their quick goodbyes before leaving, giggling amongst themselves. Phoebe wondered what was so funny but decided to focus her attention on the Sioux chief.

"So I have. Quite successful, I might add," Dan said as he stood and shook hands with Brown Bear.

"You look well, Phoebe James," Brown Bear said as he looked at the young woman who had dreamed for four nights. It was very rare that a spirit journey ever lasted more than a night and a day, but to see that she'd survived the extended journey meant that she had a good fighting spirit.

"I don't know if I honestly look well, Brown Bear, but I appreciate the compliment nonetheless," Phoebe replied between bites of food. She felt so hungry that she wasn't sure when her hunger would ever be satisfied again. Brown Bear chuckled as he focused his eyes back on Dan.

"And you, Dan Mavis, seem to have played a very important role in her spirit journey. It seemed that the moment you made it to the top, things started to progress the way they should for Phoebe James."

"I will never be able to fully explain in words what I experienced, but I am glad that it helped Phoebe. She deserves to live a life without fear," Dan said as he looked down at Phoebe, love and appreciation for her in his eyes.

"I am glad to see the two of you doing so well. I hope that your relationship together will continue to grow and that you'll both work hard to teach the children," Brown Bear said.

"Do not worry, Brown Bear. I will never abandon the children like that again," Phoebe promised.

"I will hold you to that, Phoebe James." Brown Bear then grunted his approval before departing just as many of the children started to come to the central fire to speak with Dan and Phoebe. They were eager to talk to their teachers and to learn all they could about the spirit journey that Phoebe had gone on. She shared with them bits and pieces, the more bizarre aspects of trying to get somewhere without making any progress.

"It was the strangest thing because the sun never moved in the sky, indicating how long I had been dreaming. When I woke up, I was certainly surprised to learn that I had been up there for so many days," Phoebe said to the children in Sioux.

"And it was Mr. Mavis that was your spirit guide in the end?" Squirrel asked as she looked at the schoolteacher, thinking that he didn't look all that special.

"He sure did. If it wasn't for him, I'd still be dreaming," Phoebe confirmed.

"I think you two should get married," Grasshopper then said in a very soft voice as he leaned in close to Phoebe, causing all the other children to laugh wildly.

"What did he say?" Dan asked, not having been able to hear the small boy's Sioux words.

"He thinks that what you did was very brave, entering another person's spirit journey," Phoebe said.

"Then why are they all laughing like that?" Dan countered, thinking that Phoebe wasn't being completely honest with him. But when the women came to shoo the children all away for their afternoon chores, Phoebe simply shrugged her shoulders and smiled up at Dan.

"It seems you'll have to continue your own lessons to find out," Phoebe said with a wink.

"I think that's a reasonable enough idea," Dan said as he sat back down with Phoebe on one of the many logs surrounding the central fire. They sat together and talked softly, eating whatever food was pushed into their hands. Sometimes they were asked questions about the spirit journey and Dan did his best to explain what he'd experienced, often with chuckles from the person asking the question as he continued to struggle with his Sioux.

Eventually, the day faded to twilight and Dan knew that he would need to return home to his cottage. It had been quite an experience to help Phoebe through her spirit journey, and all the Sioux people seemed to be really supportive of Phoebe for having completed it successfully. To Dan, it seemed like some sort of rite of passage that had allowed Phoebe to gain the people's utmost respect. At one point earlier in the afternoon, Dan had found his clothes once more when Edward had returned to camp. Before he left camp, he dressed in what was familiar to him, then went and found Phoebe once more to say his goodbyes.

"Have you had enough of me yet?" Phoebe asked as she placed her arms around his neck, no longer afraid to show him affection in front of so many people.

"I don't think I'll ever grow tired of you, Phoebe James, but I would like to travel home while there is still daylight to guide me," Dan explained. He leaned down and placed his lips on her forehead, giving her a brief kiss that he wished could continue longer.

"Then perhaps I'll come to town tomorrow and we can discuss the children's lessons and figure out how to influence the book club members to return," Phoebe suggested.

"Want to meet at the inn around noon for lunch and then we can go to the town hall from there to do our scheming?"

"Sounds like the perfect date," Phoebe said with a chuckle.

"Don't worry. I'll make it worth it to you," Dan said with a bright smile. Phoebe wasn't sure what he meant, but the idea excited her.

Phoebe walked with Dan to the horse corral and gave him one last embrace before he collected his horse from the herd of Indian ponies and took the time to saddle his mare. Then, he nodded at Phoebe as he rode out of the corral and Phoebe closed the thatch gate behind him. She stood there for several minutes, watching him ride away into the setting sun. Never before had Phoebe felt so much joy in her heart and anticipation in her body to see him again tomorrow.

CHAPTER 15

Dear Pa and Ma,

By the time you have received this letter, I'm confident that I'll have successfully proposed to Phoebe James. We've been courting for some time, and now that I've acquired an engagement ring, it's time to make things official. I don't know when the wedding will be, but I'm thinking sooner than later before the weather gets too cold. Every day it seems to get chillier as fall rolls right into Bear Creek.

I miss you all a bunch and hope this letter of good news warms your hearts. Tell Bethany, William, and Bobby I say hello and that I'm wishing them all well.

Sincerely,
Dan

DAN HAD JUST FINISHED WRITING his letter to his parents when Mr. Fritz came walking into the town hall late one afternoon. Dan had stayed in town, waiting for the bank to close so he could have a minute to speak with the banker. But it seemed that Mr. Fritz was taking the time to come to him, which made Dan all that more eager to know if he'd been successful.

"The package from my correspondence just came in today on the afternoon coach. As soon as I settled my affairs, I came over right away to hand over your goods," Mr. Fritz said with a smile as he approached Dan and withdrew a small, velvet box from his pocket and set it on the desk before him. Dan smiled as he took the box and opened it just a bit to confirm what was resting inside.

"Thank you, Mr. Fritz. You have been an enormous help with this whole process," Dan said as he quickly started collecting his things and stuffing them into his satchel. He wanted to get right over to Mr. Fry's to post his letter, then he needed to get out to the Jenkins'.

"It was my pleasure, Mr. Mavis. I've been contemplating the same thing with Mrs. Phillips, but I promise not to make any plans for this evening," Mr. Fritz admitted.

"Well, I look forward to hearing the good news from you sooner rather than later," Dan said as he pocketed the velvet box and slung his satchel over his shoulder before moving out from behind the desk.

"I'll be there tonight, so I look forward to seeing how things play out for you."

"Fingers crossed," Dan said with a chuckle. The two men then left the town hall and parted ways as Dan jogged across the street to the general store to have his letter posted.

"You look like you're in a hurry," Mr. Fry observed as he took Dan's money for the letter.

"Yes, I am," Dan admitted.

"Any particular reason?" Mr. Fry asked as he leaned over the counter and spoke in a soft voice.

"Oh, there sure is," Dan said with a wink. He then left the store before Mr. Fry could ask him any other questions. It would be common knowledge soon enough and figured the storekeeper would just have to be patient a little bit longer.

Dan made his way through town, eager to collect his horse and head home to get cleaned up and changed. He'd invited Phoebe and her brother Edward out to the Jenkins' ranch for a homecooked meal. Mathew had a large property with plenty of open spaces to which he could find a private moment with Phoebe. It had been Edward's idea when Dan had admitted he hadn't thought of the perfect plan yet, and he was grateful for the advice.

Once Dan made it home to his cottage, he was quick to get out of his teaching clothes and wash as thoroughly as possible before putting on his nicest suit, the one he often saved for Sunday services at the town hall. He wanted to look his best for this very special occasion, and before he left the cottage again, wanting to get to the ranch earlier, he made sure to pull the velvet box out of his other trousers and stick it in his vest pocket. Feeling the box pressed up against his chest reassured him that he wouldn't be forgetting anything.

The entire ride out to the Jenkins' ranch, Dan tried to settle his nerves. He knew that he was doing the right thing and longed to get a special moment alone with Phoebe. Everyone who was coming to the dinner tonight knew what Dan had planned and he tried to reassure himself that everything would go according to plan. Even so, he was still nervous. Despite the fact that he knew that Phoebe loved him, he couldn't seem to shake these feelings.

"Howdy there, Mr. Mavis," Peter Gibson called out to him as he rode onto the ranch. Peter was one of Mathew's cattle hands that they'd hired a few years back.

"Hello, Peter," Dan said as he steered his horse towards the barn.

"Here, let me take your mare into the barn. You just go on in and enjoy your time tonight," Peter said with a wink. Dan pulled his horse to a stop, a smirk on his lips as he dismounted and handed the reins over to Peter. It seemed like everyone was in the know tonight.

"I appreciate that very much," Dan said. Peter simply nodded, chuckling as he led Dan's horse into the barn. Taking one more deep breath, Dan made his way up the front porch of the ranch house and knocked on the door.

"It's open!" called Mrs. Phillips' voice. Dan opened the door and was pleasantly surprised by the room. A set of candles were lit on the large table that took up the space of the main room. Dan then saw Jenny and Mrs. Phillips moving about in the kitchen, a savory aroma filling the ranch house as Dan stepped in and shut the door behind him.

"Well don't you look handsome," Mathew said as he came walking in from the long hallway where all the bedrooms were situated. He carried young Mikey in his arms as the boy tried to wiggle his way to the floor. Reluctantly, Mathew set him down and Mikey began to giggle and walk around the room on his own.

"You look like you have your hands full there," Dan quipped as he shook hands with Mathew.

"He just got up from a late nap and seems to have hit the ground running. I'm thinking it's going to be a late night for all of us."

"Well, I'm certain that I won't take up too much of your time," Dan assured.

"Don't be talking silly, Dan. You take as much time as you need," Mathew replied before hurrying after his son as Mikey tried to pull down a stack of firewood next to the fireplace. A fire burned in the chimney behind the grate and Dan could see why Mathew would be concerned.

"How are you doing, my dear?" Mrs. Phillips asked as she came out of the kitchen and approached him.

"I feel like a bundle of nerves, yet I don't know why," Dan admitted.

"You got everything you need?" she asked.

"Yeah, I got the ring right here in my pocket. Edward will be bringing her by any moment now, so everything seems to be going as planned. And I know Phoebe loves me and I love her. Yet, I can't help but feel nervous," Dan explained.

"Though you have nothing to be nervous about, it's okay to be nervous. Just let the evening go and don't get too worried about anything," Mrs. Phillips advised. "And when that doesn't work, whiskey is in the cupboard." Dan chuckled with the woman who was a motherly figure to many people.

"Thank you," he said as he settled down at the table, anxious for Phoebe and Edward to arrive. When someone knocked on the door, Dan jumped in his seat, causing Mathew to laugh openly.

"Not funny," Dan said as he glared at Mathew, but he couldn't keep the smile from his lips. Mathew went to the door with Mikey in his arms, and as he opened the front door, Mr. Fritz stood on the other side holding a bouquet of flowers. As soon as Dan saw the flowers, he cursed underneath his breath. He hadn't even thought about bringing flowers for Phoebe, and with this being such an important night, he should have tried to find some wildflowers on his way to the ranch.

"Good evening," Mr. Fritz said as he came into the room and greeted everyone. Then, he handed the flowers to Mrs. Phillips, who blushed as she accepted them. It was good to see the two of them getting along well and reasoned that there would be another marriage soon after his.

"Thank you, Louis," Mrs. Phillips said as she accepted a small kiss on the cheek before she went to go find a vase to put the flowers in. Once she had finished her task, she set them on the table. "They'll make a perfect addition for tonight."

When someone else knocked on the door, Dan knew in his heart that it had to be Phoebe and Edward. He quickly stood from the table and smoothed down his vest, listening to the giggles of the women as he did so. But he didn't care and wasn't embarrassed at all. Mathew went and opened the door again, this time with Mikey hanging onto his belt as they walked together. When Mathew opened the door, a vision of an angel appeared.

There had been all sorts of dresses Dan had seen Phoebe in, from her daily simple working gowns, to the Indian maiden gown she'd worn. But never had he seen Phoebe in such an elegant gown as she stepped into the room. It was an emerald gown with the bodice trimmed in green lace. It was elegant and fitting, making Dan's heart beat even faster as she came into the house, her smile bright as ever. A black velvet necklace hung around her neck with a white brooch attached to the front. And when her eyes met Dan's, he stared into her honey colored eyes and wondered if he'd ever want to look away.

"Good evening, Miss James. Mr. James," Mathew greeted as the two siblings came into the ranch house. Dan was so mesmerized by Phoebe's appearance that he had become tongue-tied for a moment.

"Hello, Phoebe. You look lovely this evening," Dan said as he came forward and extended his hands towards her. She placed her hands in his softly and leaned her head to the side to allow him to kiss her cheek.

"Thank you. It was such a lovely ride out here. I haven't been to any of the ranches since moving to Bear Creek and I found the wide-open spaces so amazing to view," Phoebe said as she allowed Dan to seat her at the table.

"It's one of the things I love most about my cottage. It sits on a plot of land not far from town, but it's wide open in every direction. In the fall when the harvest season begins, you can see the farmers in the distance working the fields," Dan said as he sat down next to her. Edward sat across from them and winked at Dan, making him smirk. They were all eager for Dan to follow through with his plans tonight.

Light conversation presided over the room as everyone took the time to catch up and talk about the latest happenings in town. Phoebe and Dan had been able to convince the old book club members to return after hearing the real reason that Dan had started teaching the children. Someone had spread a rumor that Dan had been forced into accepting the students by the Indian chief. Once Dan explained the real reason and the goal he was trying to achieve, the book club members had agreed to come back and support Dan. In their eyes, he was helping the Indian children become more civilized and they liked that idea. Dan was just happy to have their support regardless.

"Alright, who's ready for a little surprise?" Jenny said in a cheery voice. Dan looked up to see her coming to the table with a small baking sheet with several small ramekins sitting upon it. Phoebe saw what Jenny placed on the center of the table and could hardly believe her eyes.

"You made little souffles?" Phoebe exclaimed as she placed a hand to cover her wide-open mouth in shock.

"These last few years has taught me to do a lot for myself, and when Dan mentioned how much you liked them, I figured I'd give it a shot. Had to do some practice ones with Mrs. Benning, but I like how these ones turned out," Jenny explained.

"That is so kind of you," Phoebe said, giving Dan a joyful look. "I can't believe you remembered."

"After watching how much you enjoyed eating that souffle at the inn, how could I not?" Dan teased.

Everyone ate the unique dish, commenting on how well Jenny had prepared it. And just like before, Phoebe made small sounds of pleasure as she ate hers, reliving so many happy memories. She didn't have too many of them from Boston anymore, but she could always admit that the food was one of the things she missed the most about her former life. It made her think that if Jenny could learn how to make a souffle in a remote town such as Bear Creek, then so could she. It was women like Jenny, Margret, and Rosa that really inspired a city girl such as herself to accomplish anything she put her mind to.

After they'd all finished eating and had enjoyed a slice of Margret's delicious peach cobbler, Dan stood from the table, doing his best to keep his nerves down, as he extended his hand towards Phoebe.

"Miss James, would you care to join me for a stroll around the ranch? I'm sure the sun will be setting rather soon," Dan asked.

"It would be my pleasure, Mr. Mavis," she replied in a soft voice as she took Dan's hand and allowed him to help her from her seat. Edward watched them leave, his heart full for his sister, knowing that Dan was about to make her the happiest woman in the world in that moment. As soon as the couple left the ranch house, everyone started talking excitedly about Dan finally taking the time to put his plan into action.

Hand in hand, Dan led Phoebe off the front porch and out towards one of the open fields away from the barn and the several pastures where the cattle roamed freely. The herd made sounds of greetings to them as they passed and Dan heard Phoebe chuckle as they walked.

"What's so funny?" Dan asked.

"For such large creatures, they sure seem to be friendly," Phoebe observed.

"You know, when you first came to Bear Creek, you didn't seem to be the friendliest of people," Dan mused. "You treated men like they were the plague, and since you didn't spend much time in town, you didn't have too many friends in general."

"Is there a point to this story?" Phoebe asked, pressing her elbow into his side to make him laugh.

"The point is, you've really come a long way since then. Everyone has really gotten to know you well, especially since you've started helping me with the children and teaching their lessons. It really all started once you began to attend the book club meetings. And even though men knew to stay out of your way, I think you've made plenty of good friends in both the town and up at camp. I just wanted to say how proud of you I am."

"You really mean that?" Phoebe asked, coming to a stop along the fence of one of the pastures.

"I absolutely mean it," Dan said, looking straight into Phoebe's eyes as he held onto her hand and then slowly lowered himself onto one knee. With his free hand he removed the velvet box from his vest and carefully held it up to Phoebe before flipping open the lid. "Phoebe James, I want to spend the rest of my life with you, to be with you every day and continue watching you grow into this amazing woman that I am so proud of. Will you marry me?"

"Oh, Dan, of course I'll marry you," Phoebe said as tears came to her eyes, but a wide grin formed on her lips. Dan's own smile was grand as he kissed Phoebe's hand at the knuckles and then used both hands to remove the simple diamond ring from the box and slide it onto her finger. Then he stood and quickly wrapped his arms around her, pulling her to his chest as she hugged him back. He kissed the top of her head, feeling all his anxiety and nervousness leave him now the moment had come and passed.

"Come, let's go tell everyone the good news," Dan encouraged.

"Something tells me they already know," Phoebe said in an excited voice. "But still, I can't wait." Together, they hurried back inside as the sun set, their joy and love for each other only growing with each step.

EXTENDED EPILOGUE

MARGRET COULDN'T BELIEVE the day had finally come. She'd never imagined in her wildest dreams that she'd ever marry again after she lost her late husband. She had truly loved Jenny's father, yet was so grateful to find love later in life. She stood at the door of the town hall as all sorts of chatter and talk circulated through the air. It was a chilly fall day, and the wedding had been scheduled for as soon as Pastor Munster could perform the ceremony. Now, the building was full of plenty of supporters from the town. She stood in her wedding gown, a bouquet of baby's breath in her hands.

But Margret wasn't alone. Since Pastor Munster only made it to Bear Creek once a month, Phoebe James stood at her side in her own wedding gown with a similar bouquet. Only, hers was decorated with pinecones that had been painted by the Indian children she taught with Dan Mavis. They had agreed to have their weddings together, and since neither one of them had fathers to lead them down the aisle, they figured they could be each other's escorts.

"Are you ready, my dear?" Margret asked as she turned to look at Phoebe. Her long brown hair had been teased into curls and pinned to the top of her head, exposing her long neck and beautiful jawline. Her white wedding gown had been made from silks sent all the way from Boston, a gift from her brother. Margret's own wedding gown was made from white lace and cotton, a much simpler design. And since it was Phoebe's special day as well, she didn't worry about a fancy gown.

"I'm ready as I'll ever be," Phoebe replied with a bright smile. The pianist began playing the Wedding March, and everyone in the pews stood to face the two brides. Together, they walked down the aisle carrying their bouquets, their eyes focused on the men they were about to marry.

Dan and Louis Fritz were dressed in their normal fine attire. Mr. Fritz always wore a nice suit to work at the bank, and Dan saved his best dress for services at the town hall. They had both agreed that they didn't need a brand-new suit since it was more for the women to dress in their elegant wedding gowns. Dan watched Phoebe walk up the aisle and everything around them seemed to fade away. For a moment, it was like they were dreaming again and their souls were out on another spirit jour- ney. All Dan could see was Phoebe, slowly making her way towards him.

As the women approached the altar, they passed their bouquets to Jenny, who stood by ready to take her part in the ceremony. She sat back down next to Mathew, holding the flowers and waiting to give them back after the ceremony. Phoebe and Dan stared into each other's eyes as Pastor Munster performed the ceremony. And when it was time for them to exchange their vows, they said so with pride and dedication, each wanting the other to know just how much they loved one another.

In the back of the town hall sat Brown Bear and a few of his people, to include White Raven and Standing Mountain. A few of the Indian children had attended the wedding as well with their parents. As Brown Bear watched the wedding ceremony happen, he couldn't help but feel pleased that Phoebe and Dan had finally come together. He knew that together they would help his people learn the English language and help to protect the tribe. He hadn't foreseen the deep love that would bloom between them, but he was certainly pleased that it had happened.

"You should start preparing for a wedding ceremony back at camp," Brown Bear said softly to White Raven in Sioux. He knew that not many white settlers in Bear Creek liked Indians, so he was doing his best not to draw attention to himself. He spoke very slowly and softly, as though they were in a forest and he was trying not to let the animals around him know he was nearby.

"Why do you say that?" White Raven asked in the same tone of voice.

"Now that Phoebe is married, I am sure her brother will propose to Morning Sun and make some sort of offer to her father," Brown Bear explained.

"Do you really think that Red Stag will agree to such a joining? It will be the first time that one of our people has married a white settler."

"You must remember that Edward is also half-Indian and has spent time with his own people. I think Red Stag will eventually agree. Perhaps I shall help Edward with his marriage gift for Morning Sun," Brown Bear decided.

"What do you foresee that I do not?" White Raven asked.

"I see a future for our people much unlike the life we are

living now. I'm afraid our way of life will soon be changing and fading out. The only way our people will survive is if we adapt," Brown Bear said in a very low and stern voice. He heard the medicine man sigh then, knowing that it was both true and unavoidable.

"I wish this happiness could last forever," White Raven said as he pointed to the couples that were being married.

"So do I," Brown Bear agreed, wishing everyday he could see the joining of two happy people as a sign of good things to come. But Brown Bear had a sinking feeling in his gut that things in Bear Creek were about to get troublesome.

The End

EPILOGUE

*M*argret couldn't believe the day had finally come. She'd never imagined in her wildest dreams that she'd ever marry again after she lost her late husband. She had truly loved Jenny's father, yet was so grateful to find love later in life. She stood at the door of the town hall as all sorts of chatter and talk circulated through the air. It was a chilly fall day, and the wedding had been scheduled for as soon as Pastor Munster could perform the ceremony. Now, the building was full of plenty of supporters from the town. She stood in her wedding gown, a bouquet of baby's breath in her hands.

But Margret wasn't alone. Since Pastor Munster only made it to Bear Creek once a month, Phoebe James stood at her side in her own wedding gown with a similar bouquet. Only, hers was decorated with pinecones that had been painted by the Indian children she taught with Dan Mavis. They had agreed to have their weddings together, and since neither one of them had fathers to lead them down the aisle, they figured they could be each other's escorts.

"Are you ready, my dear?" Margret asked as she turned to look at Phoebe. Her long brown hair had been teased into curls and pinned to the top of her head, exposing her long neck and beautiful jawline. Her white wedding gown had been made from silks sent all the way from Boston, a gift from her brother. Margret's own wedding gown was made from white lace and cotton, a much simpler design. And since it was Phoebe's special day as well, she didn't worry about a fancy gown.

"I'm ready as I'll ever be," Phoebe replied with a bright smile. The pianist began playing the Wedding March, and everyone in the pews stood to face the two brides. Together, they walked down the aisle carrying their bouquets, their eyes focused on the men they were about to marry.

Dan and Louis Fritz were dressed in their normal fine attire. Mr. Fritz always wore a nice suit to work at the bank, and Dan saved his best dress for services at the town hall. They had both agreed that they didn't need a brand-new suit since it was more for the women to dress in their elegant wedding gowns. Dan watched Phoebe walk up the aisle and everything around them seemed to fade away. For a moment, it was like they were dreaming again and their souls were out on another spirit journey. All Dan could see was Phoebe, slowly making her way towards him.

As the women approached the altar, they passed their bouquets to Jenny, who stood by ready to take her part in the ceremony. She sat back down next to Mathew, holding the flowers and waiting to give them back after the ceremony. Phoebe and Dan stared into each other's eyes as Pastor Munster performed the ceremony. And when it was time for them to exchange their vows, they said so with pride and dedication, each wanting the other to know just how much they loved one another.

In the back of the town hall sat Brown Bear and a few of his people, to include White Raven and Standing Mountain. A few of the Indian children had attended the wedding as well with their parents. As Brown Bear watched the wedding ceremony happen, he couldn't help but feel pleased that Phoebe and Dan had finally come together. He knew that together they would help his people learn the English language and help to protect the tribe. He hadn't foreseen the deep love that would bloom between them, but he was certainly pleased that it had happened.

"You should start preparing for a wedding ceremony back at camp," Brown Bear said softly to White Raven in Sioux. He knew that not many white settlers in Bear Creek liked Indians, so he was doing his best not to draw attention to himself. He spoke very slowly and softly, as though they were in a forest and he was trying not to let the animals around him know he was nearby.

"Why do you say that?" White Raven asked in the same tone of voice.

"Now that Phoebe is married, I am sure her brother will propose to Morning Sun and make some sort of offer to her father," Brown Bear explained.

"Do you really think that Red Stag will agree to such a joining? It will be the first time that one of our people has married a white settler."

"You must remember that Edward is also half-Indian and has spent time with his own people. I think Red Stag will eventually agree. Perhaps I shall help Edward with his marriage gift for Morning Sun," Brown Bear decided.

"What do you foresee that I do not?" White Raven asked.

"I see a future for our people much unlike the life we are living now. I'm afraid our way of life will soon be changing and fading out. The only way our people will survive is if we adapt,"

Brown Bear said in a very low and stern voice. He heard the medicine man sigh then, knowing that it was both true and unavoidable.

"I wish this happiness could last forever," White Raven said as he pointed to the couples that were being married.

"So do I," Brown Bear agreed, wishing everyday he could see the joining of two happy people as a sign of good things to come. But Brown Bear had a sinking feeling in his gut that things in Bear Creek were about to get troublesome.

The End

CAST OF CHARACTERS

- **Dan Mavis**, schoolteacher and tutor
- **Phoebe James**
- **Nancy Tender**
- Edward James, Phoebe's sister
- Mathew & Jenny Jenkins, children: Michael (Mikey)
- Margret Phillips, Jenny's mother
- Jacob & Rosa Benning, sheriff
- Tanner Williams, deputy
- Peter Gibson, cattle hand
- Bobby Lukens, cattle hand
- Mr. & Mrs. Fry, dry goods owner, seamstress
- Pastor Barthelme Munster, traveling pastor
- Mr. & Mrs. Tibet, inn owners and local restaurant/café
- Mr. Demetri Franklin, mayor of Bear Creek
- Louise Fritz, bank owner
- Curtis Denver, butcher

- Brown Bear, leader of the Sioux Indian camp
- Mitchel Franks, barber
- Dr. Harvey, local doctor
- Varies ranchers, miners, homesteaders, and the local Sioux Indians

AMELIA'S OTHER BOOKS

Montana Westward Brides

    #0 The Rancher's Fiery Bride

    #1 The Reckless Doctor's Bride

    #2 The Rancher's Unexpected Pregnant Bride

    #3 The Lonesome Cowboy's Abducted Bride

    #4 The Sheriff's Stubborn Secretive Bride

Bear Creek Brides

    #1 The Rescued Bride's Savior

    #2 A Faithful Bride For The Wounded Sheriff

    #3 The Untangling of Two Hearts

    #4 Indian Bride for the Trusty Miner

CONNECT WITH AMELIA

Visit my website at **www.ameliarose.info** to view my other books and to sign up to my mailing list so that you are notified about my new releases and special offers.

ABOUT AMELIA ROSE

Amelia is a shameless romance addict with no intentions of ever kicking the habit. Growing up she dreamed of entertaining people and taking them on fantastical journeys with her acting abilities, until she came to the realization as a college sophomore that she had none to speak of. Another ten years would pass before she discovered a different means to accomplishing the same dream: writing stories of love and passion for addicts just like herself. Amelia has always loved romance stories and she tries to tie all the elements she likes about them into her writing.

Made in United States
North Haven, CT
02 April 2025